Kaleidoscope

HANNAH MEREDITH

Singing Spring Press

This is a work of fiction. All names, characters, and incidents are the product of the author's imagination. Any resemblance to actual occurrences or persons, living or dead, is coincidental. Historical events and personages are fictionalized.

KALEIDOSCOPE

Copyright © 2014 by Meredith Simmons

ISBN: 978-0-9895641-6-8
ISBN: 978-0-9895641-7-5

Published by Singing Spring Press

For the Men in my Life—

Bob, Rob, Michael, & Will

May the Patterns of your Lives
Be Wonderful

Advent of the Patterns

Calcutta, India
1803

CAROLYN HOWE SHIFTED on the settee, scooting to the very edge so her dangling feet would touch the floor. Unlike her normal sari, her English clothes felt smothering and poked her in the oddest places. Assuming the role of the lady of the house and serving tea was worth any discomfort, however. This was the first time her father had asked her to fulfill these duties, and she wanted to make him proud.

Male voices echoed in the wide hall, and then

her father and his partner, Charles Rydell, came through the door. The men wore similar smiles. Mr. Rydell's trip to England must have been successful.

The household's majordomo Param followed, carrying the heavy silver tea service. He placed it on the table in front of Carolyn with a bow she nearly missed, since her eyes were riveted on the box their guest held. Whenever he returned from a voyage, Mr. Rydell brought her a gift. The last had been a pin shaped like a bee. She always felt grown up when she wore it. But this box was much too large for jewelry.

"Yes, Caro, this is for you." Mr. Rydell grinned, making his graying side-whiskers puff out so he resembled a lion-tailed macaque. He offered the box with a flourish. She eagerly lifted the lid to reveal a shiny brass tube mounted on a stand. It looked like a navigational instrument from a ship. "Let me," he said, lifting the device out and setting it next to the tea service on the table. "Look through here." He pointed to one end of the tube.

She dutifully placed an eye on the end piece and saw—exquisite beauty! A pattern of vivid colors glowed within. "I see a gorgeous mandala." Her voice was a reverential whisper. She'd seen many of these Hindu symbols for the universe, but none of them had shimmered with light.

"Here." Mr. Rydell moved her hand to the far end of the cylinder. "Turn this slightly and watch what happens."

Carolyn did as instructed and the shape changed into something different, but still brilliantly colored and fascinating. A long "oh" sighed from her mouth, and she rotated the tube again. A new pattern, equally vivid and entrancing, filed her vision.

Her eyes came up to meet Mr. Rydell's amused ones. "What is this called?"

"It's a kaleidoscope. A Scottish inventor came up with it, and they're all the rage in London. The name is from Greek and means something like 'to see beautiful shapes.'"

"How does it work?" she asked.

"Caro…" Her father sounded a caution. Ladies weren't supposed to be constantly curious, but she couldn't help it. How could she learn anything if she didn't ask? Mr. Rydell didn't seem to think her questions were amiss. Instead, he carefully explained about reflecting mirrors and bits of colored glass and changing patterns. She didn't fully understand what he described, but she appreciated his speaking to her as if she were an adult. Few people were willing to give a seven-year-old detailed answers.

She looked back into the kaleidoscope and watched the forms shift into new creations, each as beautiful as the last. One that looked like a butterfly took her breath away. But her hand on the end of the tube moved slightly, and the butterfly disappeared.

"Oh, it's gone. How do I make it come back?"

Mr. Rydell shook his head, his face taking on a mournful expression. "Alas, once it's gone, the exact same shape won't appear again. You might get something similar, but after a complex pattern has shifted, it won't reform. Remember, you're seeing tiny pieces of colored glass reflected in carefully aligned small mirrors. The slightest change in the position of just one of those glass pieces changes the whole."

Disappointment slumped her shoulders but didn't quell her desire to see more. She leaned toward the device.

"Caro, have your forgotten about our tea?" her father asked.

Chagrin replaced disappointment. She had indeed forgotten her duty. She must put aside the magic for the mundane. But the kaleidoscope was hers, and she could watch the changing shapes for hours, days, even years to come. All the bright, little pieces would be waiting for her to rotate the cylinder and form breathtaking new patterns.

Patterns for April 1825
London

*T*HERE WAS NO PAIN when the knife slipped between Luke's ribs, just a sharp pressure. Only when his assailant moved away, extracting the blade, did the agony hit. Luke felt warm wetness on his right side, and his knees folded like a broken toy. The cobbles rushed up to meet his face. More pain, more blood, an errant thought that he'd broken his nose—a definite loss when he traded on his looks.

Someone rolled him onto his back. Hands roamed his body, removed his pocket watch, handkerchief, the small hoard of coins inside his waistcoat. He opened his mouth to protest, but only a shallow groan emerged. His arms would not obey him. His fingers impotently rubbed the wet stone of the street.

"Ah thought ya said 'e were a toff," a voice said above him. "Scant pickins fer that."

"There's a gold 'andled cane an' a good 'at, that's worth sumpin. Git the coat, if ya dinnit muck it up. Boots look fine." A second voice, accompanied by a tugging on his carefully shined Hessians, seemed to echo from a distance.

Luke was jerked to a sitting position. The pain intensified. His blurry vision faded to black, but he could still hear the heavy breathing as a man struggled to remove his tight fitting coat and waistcoat. When his shoulders were released, his head fell back and hit the street with a force that made lights dance before his darkened eyes.

"Inta the river then," the first voice said. Powerless to resist, Luke was hauled along the cobbles like a sack of refuse. There was a strange moment of suspension, and then cold water closed over his head.

The shock roused him back to full consciousness, and he managed to move his legs enough to force his head above the lapping water. So this is death, he thought, and for so little—some well-worn clothing, a few coins, and a decent pair of boots. If the toughs had waited a few more weeks, they might have made a better haul. His one regret was that he had nothing *but* regrets. Dying was easier than living.

Luke let the water take him.

As Carolyn Rydell and her manager walked down the narrow aisles, the movement of their swinging lanterns caused shadows to career over and around the bales and crates, making it difficult to focus, turning the mundane into something fantastic. Caro would have known where she was by smell alone, however. Only a warehouse filled with products from India would be so redolent with fragrances of frankincense, patchouli, and sandalwood.

These were the scents of home, and she hated to leave them, even though the final entry in the bill of lading had been checked.

"We've finished, Memsahib," Sanjeet said softly, "and the hour is late."

"Yes, I know. I'm sorry." Caro felt a stab of guilt that she'd kept her staff so long while she indulged herself in the scents and textures that brought her comfort. This echo of her former life temporarily kept loneliness at bay, but duty called her in the here and now. "Everything can go to the sales house tomorrow," she said.

Sanjeet's teeth flashed brightly in his dark face. "And then the money will flow."

Caro smiled back at her manager. "Yes, and then all our bills can be paid." That would be a relief. The East Indiaman *Laughing Miss* had been due last month, and the ship's eventual arrival had lifted a burden from Caro's shoulders. Building and equipping a new East Indiaman put financial stress on even the consistently lucrative Rydell Shipping. At this time, the loss of *Laughing Miss*, fully loaded with expensive cargo, would have been disastrous.

Caro swept into the office to gather the rest of her retinue. Her maid Amala dozed in a chair, while the footmen, flushing with embarrassment, leaped up from a table on which sat dice and coins. The footmen provided protection; only a fool would come to the East London docks without muscle at her back.

"We're for home," she said, setting everything in motion. "Peter, inform John Coachman that we're on our way." Her elderly coachman would also be embarrassed if he were discovered napping inside the carriage, which was undoubtedly the case.

When she left the building, the breeze coming off the river felt almost cold, as if London was loath to throw off winter. In Calcutta, April would be hot and dusty. The heat was one aspect of her former home that Caro didn't miss. She inhaled the cool air, not minding the smells of rot, tar, and damp, since they accompanied the beauty of the hazy moon's reflection on the water.

She stopped abruptly when she saw what appeared to be a body nudging against the water stairs. The white of a man's shirt flickered in the moonlight. She pointed. "Sanjeet. There. Someone's in the water."

Without further direction, the small man, trailed by two bulky footmen, hurried to the water stairs and gingerly made his way down the slippery steps.

"Missy Caro, a body in the river should stay there," Amala said, her eyes huge.

"This is not the Ganges," Caro replied. "This is not a burial, but more likely murder or misadventure." She watched as her men dragged the body from the water onto the stair landing.

Sanjeet, kneeling next to the drowned man, called up to her, "He's still alive."

"Bring him," Caro called back.

"Forever you bring home injured pye-dogs," Amala grumbled. "Have you not learned that they will bite?"

"This is a man and not a feral dog," Caro said. "I think my hands will be safe.

Lord Lucien Harlington realized he was in hell. His arrival had long been predicted. Flames licked his body while demons, conversing in unknown tongues, poked and prodded at him, bringing breath-stealing pain.

Curious as always, he tried to open his eyes to see the horror that his choices in life had wrought. His body would not follow his commands, however. Perhaps part of hell's torments was that his questing mind would forever be without answers. He struggled against this constriction but was unsuccessful, until suddenly everything faded away again.

The next time Luke became conscious, he felt much cooler and was pleased to discover that his eyes now worked. He could see a canopy above him. A canopy? What was a ruffled canopy doing in hell? Was this a reminder that hell was his punishment for gazing up at too many different ladies' bed canopies in the past?

Then a face appeared in his view—a beautiful face with sharp cheekbones and dark, vaguely tilted eyes. "*Houri*," he said, reaching for her. He must have been whisked to the Muslim's heaven. How odd. He was familiar with the basic tenets from his study at university, but he definitely wasn't a believer. He didn't understand his good fortune, but the reward that any religion offered was better than the alternative. He wanted to ask the breathtaking woman how this had happened, but darkness again descended.

Caro watched the unknown man slide into

unconsciousness, confident it wasn't a precursor to death now that his fever had broken. The doctor had been right. Her inadvertent guest was now on the mend. His breathing was that of normal sleep.

"Pye-dog," Amala said at her shoulder. "I knew he would show himself to be a misbegotten cur. After saving him, he calls you a whore."

Caro smiled. Amala had been her defender since she was a child. "No, he said *houri*. I think he imagines that I'm something like an Islamic angel. Not a bad thing to be compared to."

But she suspected if there were an angel in the room, it was more probably the man on the bed. Even his battered face—the nose still swollen and the bruises now fading to a bilious yellow—could not detract from his underlying male beauty. And it was beauty more than standard handsomeness, despite his seeming to have dropped a half a stone in weight during his illness.

The sleeping man could have been the model for a sculptor, his proportions were so balanced and pleasing. Corded muscle defined his chest and abdomen. Broad shoulders tapered to a narrow waist. His legs were long and straight, his thighs powerful. And what lay between his thighs....Caro had been married for eight years but hadn't seen her husband's naked body until his last illness. Neither her husband Charles nor the Indian boys swimming in the river had prepared her for what she'd observed.

After the blood had been washed out, the injured man's hair was sandy blond, soft and silky. His eyebrows were a shade darker, as were the scattering of hairs across his chest and the surprisingly heavy beard that had formed in the past six days. His eyes, when open, were a deep blue. When closed, thick, tawny lashes lay on his bruised cheeks.

Since she'd insisted on doing the bulk of the nursing duties, Caro knew the man intimately. She knew nothing *about* him, however.

He carried no identification, but his shirt and trousers were of good quality. He had been beaten, stabbed, and doubtlessly robbed. No one had posted a notice for a missing person who resembled him. When notified, the constable had simply shrugged and said he was not his problem unless he died.

And so, her patient remained an enigma. Perhaps this was the reason Caro found the man so fascinating. She spent more hours than necessary watching him sleep. Her excuse was the beef tea she was prepared to pour in his mouth every time he showed a glimmer of consciousness. A rather weak excuse, she though with a smile.

"Missy Caro," Amala broke her reverie, "Perkins says that Lord Kelton has called. He's in the drawing room."

Caro stifled a groan. Meetings with her late

husband's nephew always irritated her. She wondered what his present complaint would be.

Water trickled between his lips—delicious, sweet water. He sucked at the wondrous elixir and opened his eyes. A hand and face jerked back from him, spilling the liquid on his chest. He followed the movement and focused on a woman. Not the *houri* he remembered. This woman was darker, older.

"Where? What?" he croaked.

The older woman looked surprised. "I'll get Missy Caro," she said in a soft, lilting voice, and withdrew from the room.

Left alone, Luke took stock of his situation. He was obviously not dead. He lay in a large bedchamber. Although the room had feminine touches, it lacked the personal accoutrements that he associated with a lady's bedchamber. A guest room, perhaps? Sunlight streamed through the windows, so he had been unconscious for the past half day.

He remembered walking toward the gambling hell where he was to meet Tremaine around one in the morning. He remembered being attacked. And then his memory became muddled.

A bandage tightly wrapped his torso, but the pain in his side was slight compared to the pounding in his head. He felt weak and lethargic, but since he was aware, he must be getting better.

The door opened, and the beautiful woman entered with the older one following closely behind. The younger woman smiled, making him feel that he was truly alive. "How do you feel?" she asked.

"Like I might live." His voice sounded rusty and worn. "Where am I? How did I get here?"

The woman sat in a chair next to the bed and took his hand in hers. It felt familiar and comfortable, a memory or a dream. "We found you in the water near the East India docks and brought you here, to my house. I'm Carolyn Rydell. And you are?"

"Luke Harlington," he said, purposely leaving off his courtesy title. He'd never seen this exquisite woman before. He would surely have remembered if he had, and he was, therefore, confident that she didn't travel in the upper level of society.

He'd heard the older woman call Carolyn Rydell "Missy Caro," so she was evidently unmarried. For this reason, as well as her startling, slightly exotic looks, and the quality of the furnishings of the room in which he lay, Luke imagined that Carolyn Rydell was some lucky man's expensive and much cherished mistress.

There was no reason to make such a woman uncomfortable knowing that she had rescued the Marquess of Greyling's youngest son. He also didn't want her running to his estranged father with his whereabouts.

As if she'd read his mind, she asked, "Is there anyone we should notify, Mr. Harlington? Someone who would be concerned about your disappearance?"

"There's no one who will have missed me, but since I'm here, it can't be said that I've disappeared." He tried to deflect her concern with humor, although it was weak humor, at best. He attempted a winning smile, but his face felt stiff and unresponsive. He raised a hand to his cheek, only to discover he'd grown a short beard. My God, how long had he been here?

"When was I found?" he asked.

"It will be a week tomorrow."

Heavens, so long! Tremaine would have assumed that Luke had changed his mind and wasn't interested in looking for the stolen gems any longer. As much as the man traveled, Tremaine might have even left London.

A knock at the door brought Carolyn's head around, but the older woman answered it. After a brief, indistinct discussion, she came up to Carolyn and said, "Lord Kelton is very disturbed by your absence and requests that you return to the drawing room."

"Oh, bother," Carolyn said, then squeezed his hand and said, "I have to go."

Luke watched her graceful movements as she

left the bedchamber. He knew the Earl of Kelton and had always thought the man a prig. He couldn't imagine that Kelton had been able to become the protector for such an exceptional woman. The thought of the delectable Miss Rydell laboring under such a fop was disgusting.

Kelton had money, however, and that must be the attraction. Not for the first time, Luke wished he hadn't alienated his father and still had a quarterly allowance.

Caro's irritation with Gerald's demands eclipsed her delight in her patient's recovery. As Earl of Kelton, Gerald evidently felt entitled to barge into her house and order her around. Open warfare was counterproductive, however, so she smothered her pique and placed a pleasant expression on her face.

"Your mystery guest has awakened, then?" Gerald held up a glass of wine as if in salute. She'd requested tea just before leaving. Unsurprisingly, he'd countermanded her order.

"Yes. And he's no longer a mystery. His name is Luke Harlington and from his speech, he's well educated. So your fears that I'd picked up some beggar off the streets were unfounded."

Gerald's face registered a number of different emotions, the primary one being shock. Some thought him handsome, although Caro could never see it. He was too soft and superficial to be appealing. With his mouth agape, he looked like a landed fish. "Lucien Harlington? You have Lord Lucien Harlington tucked away in one of your beds upstairs? Good heavens, woman. Have you no concern for the family name?"

Caro didn't care about her effect on the Rydell name. According to Gerald, both her heritage and her adherence to trade had already damaged the family's social standing. This current objection, however, made no sense. "If you're correct as to the man's identity, I don't see how my rescuing a peer can be seen as negative."

His floppy mouth tightened into a sneer. "In this case, *lord* is a courtesy title. Harlington's father is the Marquess of Greyling, but there is nothing noble about Lucien. His deviant behavior is such that even his father has cast him off. He's scandalous in the extreme. And you have him staying in your home without a chaperone in residence. I hope even *you* can see the negative in this."

She knew laughing would be like poking a hornet's nest, but the sound leaked out despite her efforts. "The man has been grievously injured and isn't mobile. Hardly a threat to anyone's virtue. And then, I'm a widow nearing thirty years of age, not some virginal debutant in need of a chaperone. Amala is in attendance at all times, anyway."

"Society would never consider some Indian

servant a chaperone. Everyone will only see that you've opened your home to a whoremonger—and assume you're taking advantage of his experience since, as you've said, you're a mature widow." He suddenly stood and came over to lean on the arms of her chair. His mouth formed a rictus of disgust. "You're lucky my mother and I allowed you to use our name when you landed on our doorstep. We doubt that Uncle Charles ever married you. It makes more sense that you were his mistress and somehow got a sick old man to will you the controlling interest in a successful shipping firm."

Caro brought her hand up and shoved Gerald hard in the chest. At the same time, she hooked a foot behind his right calf and pulled forward. Unprepared, he toppled backwards and landed on his butt—hard. She stood and leaned over his prone figure. "I've always been embarrassed that a man as good as Charles Rydell was related to *you*. I keep hoping that since you use your title, no one will realize there's a connection. Because you're a very stupid man. Charles had nothing in his will that said you and your mother should get a percentage of the profits from Rydell Shipping. I did that in an effort to buy your acceptance, but I told you Charles had made these arrangements to salve your pride. Well, since I've received nothing but your disdain, no more money will be coming."

She swiveled and walked away.

"Where do you think you're going?" he asked.

"Why, upstairs to talk with the only gentleman in the house. And if I'm lucky, maybe he'll show me what has made him infamous."

Luke hadn't expected the woman to return so quickly. She flew into the room with bright flags of agitation showing on her cheeks. Her pupils covered nearly all her irises, making her dark eyes black. Anger rolled off her like steam from a boiling kettle. She'd obviously had words with her protector. A spurt of guilt shot through him and prompted his saying, "I hope my presence here hasn't caused you to argue with Lord Kelton and lose what is obviously a financially lucrative position."

She stopped mid-stride. "Excuse me?"

Was she embarrassed that he'd guessed she was Lord Kelton's mistress? When Luke was young and still had the funds, he'd kept a bouncy brunette named Holly, and she'd seemed proud of her position. Of course, she'd been prouder still when she moved on to being the mistress of a viscount. Even when Luke had received an allowance, it hadn't been princely.

"I made the assumption that you were Kelton's, eh..." he searched for inoffensive euphemism, "very good friend and that he was financially supporting you."

"You thought that I was that idiot Gerald's mistress?" She grinned and then laughter bubbled out. Once she started, she seemed unable to stop, leaning over and pressing her hands against her mouth. He tried to get up. She noticed the motion and waved him back, pulling in great gulps of air.

"I'm sorry," she said when she was again in control of herself. "But that was the funniest thing I've heard in some time. I wouldn't become Gerald's mistress if I were starving, and he wouldn't want me if I were a gift."

She'd said that Kelton was an idiot, and he'd have to be one if he weren't interested in Carolyn Rydell. With her face flushed and her dark eyes glittering, she was magnificent. It took very little imagination to visualize her stretched across a bed with her raven's wing hair rioting on the pillow. And the lower portion of Luke's anatomy didn't lack for imagination. He sat up straighter in bed to hide his obvious interest. His head and side still ached, but he was assuredly not dead. "I can't believe there's a man alive who would not want you," he blurted out before his brain could stop his mouth.

She laughed again, but this time the sound was companionable and appealing. "Gerald has never forgiven me for having an Indian grandmother and for marrying his uncle. To have someone of my heritage in his esteemed family is anathema and, more importantly, if I didn't exist, the income from the Rydell Shipping Company would be his now that his uncle has died. So the two of us do not rub along well together."

Luke was surprised he hadn't equated the Rydell family name with the Earl of Kelton's family. But Kelton had come to his title when he was only a boy and in Luke's remembrance, had always simply been Kelton. That Carolyn—no he must think of her as Mrs. Rydell—was a widow explained why there was no husband or father in evidence. "I can see why the two of you don't get along. I must admit that I never much liked the man."

She chuckled again. "Well, it seems he's not too fond of you either. In speaking of you, among his many descriptive phrases was 'whoremonger.'"

This had to be one of the oddest conversations he'd ever had with a lady, for Mrs. Rydell was every inch a lady, regardless of how plain spoken she was. No, not just plain spoken. In her unbridled mirth and uncensored word choices, Mrs. Rydell sounded like a man.

"I take exception to that description. I've never consorted with whores," he said, echoing her forthright language. Of course, he had consorted elsewhere, but that wasn't the point. "I will admit, however, that among the ton, my reputation is perhaps not all that it could be." Now that was the greatest understatement that had dropped from his lips for all time.

"So I was led to believe. Gerald's advice was that I throw you out as quickly as possible if I hoped to retain the minimal acceptance in society that I have."

Guilt, his persistent friend, asserted itself again. "Kelton is an ass, but in this he's correct. My being here can do your reputation no good." If her grandmother were indeed an Indian, then Carolyn Rydell was clinging to respectability by her fingertips. It might have been different if her husband had been alive or if Kelton had enthusiastically embraced her as family, but this didn't seem to be the case. Society was not kind toward those they deemed half-casts. Having been its recipient, he was well aware of the cruelty lurking in London drawing rooms.

"I doubt you could injure my reputation, and that's hardly a consideration since I seldom go out in society as it is." She came over by the bed and began fussing with his pillows. He breathed in her elusive, spicy scent and knew she would not be welcomed in many drawing rooms simply because of her beauty. The ladies of the ton didn't relish imported competition.

"You should go out in society. Nothing protects a woman like marriage to a peer, and I can't imagine that there are not a number who would happily marry you."

She gave him a rueful smile. "I'm well aware of this concept. My late husband married me to give me the protection of his name. Since I arrived in London a year ago, I have not been without offers. But the men who offered marriage were impoverished, and the attraction was my wealth and not myself. Men with plenty of money made *other* offers."

Luke bet they did. And he suspected even those who needed funds were motivated by more than the desire for financial improvement. He knew he would have been. "Are you quite wealthy, then?" he asked.

"Quite." She dropped her eyes as if embarrassed, long black lashes fanning her cheeks.

"Then this makes my departure even more imperative. I'm afraid I fall into the 'impoverished' category, and I've been known to take gifts from women." The admission was harder than he'd anticipated. He wanted her good opinion, even if he didn't deserve it.

"Why don't you then take employment?" She seemed perplexed. "I have never understood men who complain about their poverty and do nothing to change the situation."

He nearly laughed. She obviously didn't have a good opinion of him, but it wasn't because he accepted presents from women. She thought he should be gainfully employed, and he could hardly claim his talent in the bedroom was his vocation.

"Laziness," he admitted. "While my father covered my bills, it was easier simply to enjoy life. And then, after my fall from grace, I did attempt to obtain a suitable paying position. I applied to various gentlemen for the position of secretary. My education made me well-qualified for this work, but my reputation ensured that no one would hire me. As some of your thwarted suitors were undoubtedly trying to do, I could marry money, but so far, I've been unable to make myself take that route." He didn't go on to say that he couldn't imagine a lifetime with any of the woman who would settle for him.

"I think this aversion to work is a peculiar trait of the British upper class." She smiled to take the sting out of her words. "Are you actually in debt? If so, I could hire you as a clerk in one of my warehouses."

"No, not in debt. Thank God. But reduced to frugality and relying on the kindness of friends." He had a distinct vision of himself as a clerk, one of the many drones who flitted about town on their masters' business. The idea was appalling. He was more of a snob than he liked to admit. "And I've relied on your kindness for too long. I have a friend, Viscount Tremaine, who will come collect me if he's still in town."

He didn't want to leave but feared that if he stayed, he'd end up a clerk in a warehouse just to be near Carolyn Rydell. Something about her called to him in ways he didn't understand. He saw a vulnerability beneath her brisk competence that he recognized in himself. It was well past time he left.

Caro stood at the window and watched as Lord Lucien's friend awkwardly helped him into the carriage. She'd said her good-byes in the foyer. Hovering on the doorstep like a sailor's wife waiting for the ship to leave would be demeaning. So, she'd kept her self-respect intact but couldn't resist peeking around the curtain until the carriage disappeared from sight. Lord, she hated to see him leave. Knowing he was lying in bed upstairs had somehow made her loneliness less evident.

And she was willing to confess she was lonely. She usually stayed so busy she didn't notice, but with Luke's departure, the house was once more echoingly empty. She would again stay late at the shipping office and bring work home with which to fill the evening hours. She could have brief conversations with Amala, but she had long grown away from the girl Amala recognized. She found herself exhausted from maintaining her youthful persona if they talked too long.

She missed Charles. She missed India. Life there was not always perfect, but it had been filled with patterns she recognized and found comfortable.

Coming to England might have been a mistake, but she'd promised Charles she'd relocate here. She hadn't fit into Anglo-Indian society, which had begun excluding those with Indian blood, and Charles had thought that when he was gone, she could come to England and start anew. He'd imagined that her connections to an earl's family would make her mixed heritage less important. Charles had also stressed that she had people she could trust to handle the Calcutta end of the business and that the weakest connection was in London.

Neither she nor Charles had imagined that his nephew and the rest of the family would be so resistant to her arrival, however. Their hostility had made her acceptance nearly impossible. She was determined to make a place regardless of their attitudes—but it was hard.

She wanted to hear Charles' beloved voice again. Unconsciously, her hand reached out and stroked the smooth surface of the kaleidoscope he'd given her so long ago. It made her feel close to him and was a symbol of his many kindnesses. She leaned over and peered through the ocular. Rotating the cylinder, she watched the patterns change. Each form was predictably unpredictable—each shape different, yet still beautiful.

But how she wished she could return to the patterns of old.

Patterns for May 1825

*L*UKE LEANED OVER THE HAND-DRAWN floor plan and pointed to the east wall of his half-brother Templeton's office. "The safe is there, behind a panel to the right of the fireplace. The panel opens by pushing on the right side." He looked up at Tremaine's lowered head. "You're sure this locksmith you know can pick a safe?"

Tremaine gave him a gleeful smile. His friend seemed to relish all this plotting. Tremaine's attitude and his ability to quickly produce a dishonest locksmith gave credence to the rumors that the older man had done something clandestine in the war with Napoleon. By comparison, Luke, who'd initiated the harebrained idea, was a nervous mess.

"Sharp can pick it, as long as you're sure it's there," Tremaine said.

"Lord help us. Your lock pick is named Sharp?"

"It's what I've always called him." Another cheeky grin appeared.

"Well, I know the safe is there. Before I became *persona non grata*, father sent me to Templeton's to have some family papers stored there. Temp was happy to show off his new safe, which he'd had installed behind a false wall in an opening next to one of the large chimneys. Father, at least, was convinced this was more secure than the safe at his house. So, if my mother's jewels are anywhere, that's where they should be."

"But you're not sure they're there?"

"No." That was the wrinkle in the plan.

His father hadn't summoned him until his mother lay dying. He'd been appalled at her skeletal appearance, her wheezing breath. Regret closed his own throat. He should have forced the issue and insisted on seeing her when he'd first heard she was ill. But his pride, his damned arrogant pride, had kept him from begging entry into a house where the door had been locked against him. Until it was too late for any true rapprochement.

He'd lifted his mother's hand and gently kissed the parchment dry skin that clung tightly to the bones.

Her pale blue eyes opened. "Lucien?"

"*Oui, ma mere.*"

"The marriage settlement is clear. The jewels are yours."

And then her eyes closed and she slept. She never reawakened.

His father couldn't ban him from a funeral at which he was a chief mourner, but afterwards, when he asked about the loose stones his mother's family had brought with them from France during the Terror, he was met with a blank stare. "She long ago sold them to aid other émigrés," his father said and walked away.

Luke knew his father lied. At the time, with his supposed disgrace still fresh, he'd assumed his father withheld the gems as part of his punishment. But his father had continued to deny the jewels' existence—as if Luke had not played with them as a boy. As if, when he was grown, his mother had never mentioned them as his legacy protected by her marriage settlement.

Well, enough was enough. He would simply take what was his. He'd already been delayed over a month due to his injuries.

"Will everything be in place for the night of the Hazelton's ball?" he asked Tremaine.

"The Earl of Kelton requests a moment of your

time." Sanjeet's delivery was bland, but his eyebrows were raised in the question his inflection didn't indicate. As manager of Rydell Shipping, Sanjeet shared Carolyn's enmity with her late husband's nephew. He'd strutted around the office for days when he learned she'd put Kelton on the floor with the hook-and-push trick he'd taught her.

But what was Gerald doing here? He never came to the Rydell Shipping offices. He preferred to pretend the shared name was happenstance, since the family of a peer wouldn't be involved in crass commerce. He'd appreciated the monthly stipend this commerce generated, of course. Its withdrawal had probably prompted his visit.

Carolyn hadn't seen him in nearly a month, not since their argument at her house. Before his death, her late husband Charles had suggested giving some money to that side of the family to make them more amenable to easing her way into London society. The idea had been a good one; it just hadn't worked. Charles would have been the first to tell her to stop a bribe when it didn't have the desired effect.

"Where is he?" she asked.

"In the outer office."

"Good. Keep him away from anything with numbers on it and give me five minutes to put the ledgers away here. Then bring him up."

Sanjeet nodded and left as she methodically stacked the ledgers in the deep bottom drawer of her desk. She suspected Gerald wouldn't have any interest in the company's profits and losses, but Charles had taught her to guard all financial information. She was sitting at the desk with a three-year-old bill of lading in front of her when Gerald entered.

"Lord Kelton, what brings you here?" She definitely wasn't going to say it was a pleasure to see him. She was done with polite lies.

"I called at your house a few times, and you were not at home."

And to him, she never would be, but that was unnecessary to say, even in the service of honesty. "Is there a reason for your diligence in hunting me down?" She remained seated, but didn't offer him the same courtesy.

"I had an interesting conversation with Dr. Grumman a few days ago. He's retired now, but still frequents our club." He looked at her expectantly. Caro had no idea who Grumman was, but since Gerald was obviously so pleased with meeting him, she was sure she wouldn't like the man.

"And..." She waited for the rest of his revelation.

"He's been the Rydell family doctor for years. He was reminiscing about the last time he saw Charles, which must have been a dozen years ago on his last voyage home. When I told him Charles's widow was here, he was very surprised. It seems that Charles went to Dr. Grumman about impotence caused by some tropical disease he'd contracted. And Grumman diagnosed the problem as untreatable."

Caro came to her feet. "This is not a topic one discusses with a lady. I think you should leave."

"Oh, I think this is an excellent topic to discuss with my late uncle's so-called widow. I could imagine an old man wanting a mistress like you to revive his failing masculinity, but now that I know he was incapable of consummation—"

"Out!" She imperiously pointed toward the door.

Instead, he slouched into a chair with a smarmy grin. "Why should I leave the office of a company that will soon be mine? You can wave that phony Indian marriage certificate around all you want, no English court is going to believe Charles Rydell actually married someone like you when he couldn't even bed you. My attorney is confident that we can prove you're the charlatan that mother and I have always known you to be."

"You are crude and uncouth. You have no idea what a real marriage is like. Rydell Shipping will never be yours. Leave now!" She raised her voice. "Sanjeet!"

The small Indian's head popped through the door so fast that it was obvious he had been hovering just outside. "Get some men to escort this man out and make sure he is never again admitted."

Sanjeet nodded and disappeared. Gerald came to his feet and sauntered to the door. "I can see myself out. Enjoy your little piece of power. It won't be yours much longer."

The two large footmen who traveled with her to the dock area arrived but stood aside as Gerald did, indeed, see himself out. Caro subsided back into her desk chair. "Close the door," she said. She didn't look up until she heard the latch click and knew she was alone. Then she let the tears come.

None of these cold, emotionless people on this cursed island would ever understand what her marriage to Charles had been like. She'd loved him. It was that simple.

She'd been fourteen when her father had senselessly died in a bridge collapse. She'd been lost, adrift—and Charles had been there for her. A surrogate father. A guide through the labyrinth of Anglo-Indian society. A mentor who taught her to take her father's place at Howe & Rydell Shipping.

They'd married when she was seventeen after a disreputable young officer, attracted primarily by her wealth, had attempted to compromise her. Charles had already been ill with a combination of debilitating diseases, the curse of a European too long in the tropics, and had thought their time together would be short-lived. He'd hoped to protect her by giving her the status of his wife. He had seen, even then, that the East India Company would soon rule all of India, and the more English she seemed, the safer her future would be.

As it turned out, they had eight years together—years that had seen her grow in experience and confidence. Years that had seen her slowly take control of the company now called simply Rydell shipping. Happy years.

Charles had explained from the first that they could not truly live as man and wife and had often expressed his guilt that he'd taken so long in dying. He felt he'd stolen her youth. But Caro saw their marriage as time well spent. Yes, she'd loved him—and missed him horribly.

She'd never imagined that anyone would discover their marriage had not been consummated, however. This information was personal and private. Information that if bandied about would demean Charles's memory.

Tight fear twisted her gut. Would the fact that she and Charles hadn't enjoyed marital relations void her marriage? She had no idea if this would make any difference in English law. She recalled reading the phase "wedded and bedded" somewhere, but she thought that applied to marriages in the distant past. Would her persistent virginity negate an actual ceremony? Dear Lord, could Gerald insist she be examined by a physician? The thought sickened her.

Perdition! This sniveling behavior was counterproductive. As with all problems, she would attack this head-on. She pulled a crisp handkerchief from her reticule and blew her nose in a great honking, unladylike sound that echoed in the empty office and made her mouth curl into an ironic smile. She would never be an English lady—really hadn't wanted to be one. She knew she'd never fit into society and had been content to live on the fringes.

But she was smart and not without her own area of influence. Ships sailed the world at her command. Because of her decisions, products from one continent were sold on another half a world away. She had money. She had beauty. There was no need to pretend false modesty when her mirror and men's reactions told her the latter was true.

She would use her assets to fight the Earl of Kelton—and she would win. She would grind his haughty face into the dust of the street. All he had was the word of some ancient family doctor that Charles had been incapable of physically being her husband. She could easily eliminate the evidence of this fact. She simply had to find a discrete partner to relieve her of her long held virginity. The rest was the territory of lawyers, and she could hire the best. She suspected Gerald and his whey-faced mother would run out of money long before she did and have to retire from the field.

She only had to adjust the settings a little and the patterns would change. She smiled and began to make her plans.

Luke surveyed the ballroom. Tomorrow's papers would proclaim the Hazelton's ball a great success. Everyone with even the pretense of being anyone was there. When his half-brother discovered the theft, Luke would be the immediate suspect, but he would have the entire ton to testify he had been dancing the night away.

He planned to make himself obvious by asking a number of debutants to dance. The chaperones of these virginal misses would be aghast, but the girls themselves would eagerly add his name to their dance cards. Nothing was as attractive as the forbidden—and he was confident most had been warned against him. After all, he was the bounder who had compromised Lady Belinda Fuquay and then refused to marry her.

Lady Belinda had named him as the father of the child she carried, and everyone took her word as the truth. Since he'd only conversed with her on two occasions, and never alone, he wasn't sure how this miraculous conception was supposed to have taken place. But no one had believed his protestations of innocence. No lady would admit to such ruin if it weren't true.

He had no idea why she'd chosen him. Perhaps because he was studying for the church at the time and she imagined him so filled with the milk of human kindness that he would happily make a nest for both her and her burgeoning cuckoo. Lady Belinda hadn't taken into account that the son of an English marquess and a French countess would have too much pride to be a dupe.

He'd lived to regret not marrying her. How could he have suspected that desperation would lead Lady Belinda to hang herself in her dressing room? Her false accusation and suicide had alienated him from his family, rendered him unfit for the clergy, and set him firmly on the path to becoming a wastrel.

But, ironically, notoriety carried its own allure, and he continued to be invited to most of society's events. He was tolerated as long as he restricted his perceived predatory behavior to those widows and bored wives of the fast set. Tonight, he would prowl the debutants, however, and *that* would be remembered.

He could only hope that Tremaine and his tame safecracker would find his mother's unset jewels in his eldest brother's safe. The infusion of such wealth would enable him to buy a small stud farm somewhere in a distant county. There he could make himself into a different person. Perhaps he could become someone he liked better than he did his present self.

He had the will to change. He just needed the means.

He greeted his host and hostess, then headed unerringly toward the cluster of pale gowns that delineated tonight's quarry. His steps slowed at the sound of laughter from a cluster of men to his right. Two of the men shifted so he could see the object of their interest—a shapely woman in brilliant green. Ladies dressed in bright colors weren't his present goal, but his feet unconsciously turned in that direction.

Between the bodies of the adoring group, Luke caught only quick flashes of the surrounded lady. Hair as dark as night arranged in an elaborate design. A long, graceful neck. Gently sloping shoulders. Skin the color of weak tea with milk. Intermittent shimmers of fine silk that sparkled like green fire. And then the lady turned, and he gazed into the fathomless depths of Carolyn Rydell's dark eyes.

He was surprised that he was *not* surprised. It seemed that he had known from the first that it was she. The men between them seemed to melt away like wax in the sun. He bent over her hand and kissed it. "Mrs. Rydell."

One of her dark brows arched slightly, but she too seemed unsurprised at his arrival, almost as if this meeting had been planned or inevitable. "Lord Lucien. I'm delighted to see you looking so well."

"I didn't realize you two were acquainted." Templeton's dry, disapproving voice broke into what had seemed to be a private conversation. Interesting. His oh-so-married, elder half-brother was one of the swarm gathered around Carolyn Rydell. His middle brother David would have been less of a surprise, since David had married for money and found his amusement elsewhere. Temp, however, had always seemed to adhere to the straight and narrow. Luke kept his face composed, but inwardly he smiled. He wouldn't have to worry about having a firm alibi for the robbery that was, hopefully, taking place at this very moment at Templeton's house.

"Mrs. Rydell was the good Samaritan whose servants plucked me from the Thames when I was accosted last month." Luke turned his attention back to Carolyn, as Templeton mumbled something about low places. "I hope you have a place for me on your dance card. Perhaps the supper dance?" He suddenly very much wanted to spend time with this intriguing woman. His sexual desire must have been as battered as his body while he was in residence in her home. He remembered her only with kindness and not the lust that was currently roaring through his blood.

She examined the card that dangled from her wrist. "Alas, that dance is Lord Penhurst's, but the first set after supper is open."

Well into the evening. No doubt a quadrille. Not even a waltz. Disappointment rode him, but Luke dutifully signed his name and took his leave. At least his presence was established and he would not have to terrorize any of the young misses and their mothers. With relief, he headed toward the card room.

Tremaine found him there an hour later. The look on his friend's face told him everything, but he still excused himself and met Tremaine at the side of the room.

"No loose gemstones in your brother's safe," Tremaine immediately said.

"Half-brother."

The older man waved away the objection. "Semantics. We found a lot of papers that indicate Templeton has made some well-paying investments in shipping, an emerald necklace I remember his wife wearing for years, and a small packet of bank notes. I took a few odd bills to pay Sharp for his time, but left everything else. We buttoned everything up, and it's possible Templeton will never know the safe was opened."

"What about the missing money?"

Tremaine laughed. "I doubt your *half*-brother counts his coins as carefully as you do. This was just cash on hand, and he probably doesn't know the exact amount he's put in there. But I'm damned sorry we didn't find your legacy."

"As am I." Just saying the words pierced him with loss. He'd allowed himself to hope, to imagine another life. He'd been so damned sure the jewels would be in the safe. He again saw the gems tumbling through his own boyish hands, catching the light and making him laugh at the sparkling patterns they made. He knew his mother had owned them then, and she'd mentioned the jewels at the end. His father had to be wrong about their being used to help other French émigrés.

"But what are you doing hiding in the card room? I thought the idea was to make yourself conspicuous by dancing with the debutants."

"I ran into Templeton early on, so he knows I'm here. I decided to spare those making their come-out. Right now I'm just killing time until I can claim my dance."

An incredulous look froze Tremaine's mobile face. "Good God, Luke. You're on someone's dance card? This is taking conspicuous behavior to the limit. Who's the unfortunate chit?"

"No chit. Mrs. Rydell."

"Your delectable rescuer is here? Now there's someone I wouldn't mind standing up with myself."

The use of the word *delectable* irked Luke. "I'd prefer if you didn't," he said in a tight voice.

Tremaine grinned and slapped him on the back. "Not a bad plan. Your Mrs. Rydell has the worth of more than a few bags of gems in her possession— and the packaging is superb. You'd come out much better than your half-brother David did when he married for coin."

Luke hadn't thought of Carolyn in those terms. He'd simply wanted to dance with her. To again feel her small, soft hand in his, to again see a smile in her dark eyes. And he'd do so as soon as the interminable supper ended.

The pall of disappointment over not finding the jewels loosened its grip on his shoulders and floated away.

Caro was sure she was developing a tic in her right cheek. She'd spent the entire evening smiling at idiots, and the false, frozen expression was taking its toll. As with her earlier forays into English society, she was surrounded by men interested in either marrying her money or enjoying an illicit tumble in the sheets. As examples of British manhood, she found them universally wanting. There certainly wasn't a discrete lover in the entire group. Actually, she couldn't envision any one of them as a lover, discrete or otherwise.

While she lacked experience, Caro was not without knowledge. No one who grew up in India could be ignorant of what went on between men and women. She'd spent hours studying the carvings on temples and trying to reconcile the basics she knew to the convoluted couplings illustrated in stone. Much of this still eluded her, although she well remembered the heady rush when that young officer had kissed her in the garden. But then he'd grabbed her and squeezed her breasts. She'd been frightened and was trying to push him away when Charles found them. She'd fled to Charles's encircling arms and felt safe there.

Charles's embrace had been filled with the sweetness of coming home. But before it had gone so wrong, the young officer's kiss had been like running down a steep hill, knowing that at any moment she could fall, but enjoying the exhilaration of the danger. If she were going to rid herself of her virginity, then she wanted the fervor she'd briefly experienced. She didn't feel even a glimmer of this emotion for anyone in the milling crowd of men around her.

And then she saw Lucien Harlington coming toward her, weaving his way through the throng like a tiger stalking prey through the forest. He was all controlled power and subtle grace. Something within her whispered *maybe*.

Luke wasn't frightening. He was a known quantity. As he lay injured in her house, she'd watched him and had held his hand when fever terrors haunted his mind. She was comfortable with him. Yet something pulsed beneath the surface. *Maybe*?

"I believe this is my dance," he said, gently taking her hand and separating her from the herd.

In that brief space of privacy as they walked to take their places in the waiting set, she could feel the beat of his pulse where her fingers rested on his wrist. The scent of clean male—and something more—surrounded him and called to her. *Maybe* became *yes*.

She leaned toward him and quietly asked, "Could you call on me tomorrow morning, well before visiting hours?"

He was the one to utter the word she'd been thinking. "Yes."

Changes in the Patterns for May 1825

CARO PACED THE DRAWING ROOM and wondered if she were a fool. What had seemed sensible and inevitable beneath last night's flickering candles appeared ridiculous and impossible in the light of day. Oh, she had no doubt that Lord Lucien would be happy to make her his mistress. Even the little she knew of his reputation assured her of this.

She also knew how to interpret men's speculative looks—and last night as they'd danced, Luke's gaze had fairly smoldered. She was confident he'd agree to the physical aspects, but was less sure of his reaction on learning that she only required his services on one occasion and that secrecy was paramount.

Even though she knew he was short of funds, she didn't think he'd respond well if she offered him money. That would definitely change the dynamics. Despite her amusement when he'd initially assumed she was Gerald's mistress, Carolyn doubted Luke would react similarly if their positions were reversed. Anger and rejection seemed his more likely response.

Unable to sleep, she was up before dawn. Her mind struggled to find the best way to negotiate—for this would be a negotiation just as surely as the effort needed to arrive at a price for a shipment of Chinese silk. Last night at the ball, she'd dressed for seduction, but this morning, she'd donned her usual office attire—a severe, dark blue dress best suited for a governess. She wanted this to happen, but on her terms. She needed to remain as aloof and businesslike as possible.

She suspected her erratic pulse and shortness of breath were the result of more than just the normal nerves that arrived before she began to bargain. She didn't just want this to happen—she specifically wanted it to happen with him, Lord Lucien Harlington.

She'd relegated him to the back of her mind after he'd left her house, combatting the persistent loneliness with dutiful work, dropping into bed late at night when exhaustion claimed her. Until she'd seen him last night, she hadn't realized how she missed him. Without question, Luke was a breathtakingly handsome man, but what she'd first noticed when he approached her at the ball was his aura of familiarity. She'd wished all of the others had disappeared so she could be alone and comfortable with Luke.

She attempted to look over the budget for proposed changes to the new ship, but the figures kept slipping out of their columns and made no sense. Her attention was too fixed on the sound of a horse or carriage arriving—and so far, none had. She got up to wander the room, carefully avoiding the windows that fronted on the street. She didn't want to appear too anxious. She trailed her hand across the spines of books in the case until she came to the kaleidoscope sitting in its frame.

She carefully swiveled the end cap, knowing she'd changed the pattern within. But this time, she was too keyed up to look in the ocular to see what she'd wrought.

Would he never come?

Luke had dressed with exceptional care. He chose not to examine his desire to look impressive. Well, as impressive as was possible in clothing that was not quite the first stare of fashion. He regretted the loss of his best boots to the brigands who'd attacked him, but he'd spent this early morning bringing his second best pair to a brilliant shine. He was as ready as he ever would be. Taking a deep breath, he dropped the doorknocker.

The butler who answered gave Luke a smile of recognition, but the man seemed only vaguely familiar. When Luke thought back on his time in this house, his mind saw a play of shadows. He remembered only Carolyn Rydell in vivid colors.

"Lord Lucien Harlington to see Mrs. Rydell," Luke said, handing the man his card. Luke wasn't sure why she had asked him to visit her, but he wanted to present his most proper persona regardless of the reason.

"She's expecting you, Lord Lucien. If you will follow me."

As the butler moved off, Luke touched his arm, stopping him. "I'm sorry I don't recall your name."

"Perkins, milord. When we were first introduced, you were insensate."

"But we were introduced?" Luke couldn't imagine any scenario where anyone would introduce a comatose man.

"To an extent." Perkins suddenly grinned broadly. "I helped the footmen haul you upstairs. You are a very heavy man."

With a slight chuckle, the butler turned and ascended the stairs, leaving Luke nothing to do but follow. He wondered what besides his weight the man knew about him. The question left him feeling even more uncertain.

This nagging disquiet increased when he entered a drawing room filled with bouquets of flowers. If their number were any indication, Mrs. Rydell would be inundated with male callers later in the day. To his chagrin, none of the flowers were from him. Had he been remiss in not sending even a small nosegay?

Carolyn must have read this thought on his face, since she rose from a chair near the windows with a low laugh. "Yes, it is a bit overwhelming, but it seemed such a waste not to display them—and I do enjoy flowers."

Carolyn liked flowers. Luke tucked that piece of information into the back of his mind, although until he found his mother's jewels, he wouldn't be able to afford such abundance. Perhaps he could sneak out at night and denude half the gardens in London... He shook his head at his errant thoughts. "I'm sure the florists of London appreciate you. Does this happen every time you go out into society?"

"I'll not sound properly modest if I say yes, but this is fairly typical." She motioned to the chair across from hers. "Please be seated, Lord Lucien. You've now discovered one of the reasons I so seldom attend large balls."

Luke waited until she was again settled before he too sat down. "You led me to believe you weren't well-accepted in society."

Her smile was rueful. "I'm accepted by only certain segments. If I were to be here for visiting hours today, I doubt I would have any ladies coming to call."

"You won't be at home?"

Her smile widened, and he could see the remnants of an impish child peeking out of that expression. "Oh, no. I'll be toiling away at Rydell Shipping, and none of my supposed suitors will come there. Perkins will tell them where I am, and nothing will depress their ardor more than being reminded that my wealth not only comes from trade, but that I actually work. And so I will get to enjoy these lovely blossoms and not have to contend with their senders."

"It would seem less of a bother to simply buy your own flowers."

"But not nearly as satisfying."

Carolyn did, indeed, look pleased with her flower-gathering gambit. Luke's mouth also curved into a smile, and most of his nervousness dissipated. "Did you manage to extract a bouquet from my brother?"

"Your brother?"

"Yes, the Earl of Templeton is my eldest half-brother. He was buzzing around you last night."

She paused, as if mentally cataloguing her tributes. "The pink roses, I believe." She waved her hand in the direction of a massive arrangement near the door. "But I hadn't realized the relationship. Even after a year in London, I can't keep the titles straight. I'm afraid I'm no good at gossip, since I can't remember who is related to whom."

"Which may be why you are not so popular with the other ladies, since that seems to be the bulk of their conversation." A shadow flickered across her face, and Luke realized that what he'd thought a clever riposte was instead a reminder of the prejudice against her. "But I'm sure you asked me here for some other purpose than to flaunt your flowers."

He'd hoped to change the subject, but even that hadn't come out quite as he'd intended. Her mobile face stilled and became a serious mask. "Yes, I had another purpose. I need to ask a favor of you."

Luke leaned forward, elbows on his knees. He hoped he looked as serious as Carolyn did. "My dear lady. After what you did for me, if it is within my power to grant, anything you desire will be yours."

She frowned and looked away. What terrible thing could she be contemplating? Luke may have planned a burglary, but he'd never done anything else that was illegal. For Carolyn Rydell, however, he would consider anything except murder. And perhaps even that, given the right circumstances.

Her eyes suddenly returned to his, and she stared at him with incredible intensity, as if she were trying to see into his soul. "I want you to rid me of an inconvenient virginity."

With difficulty, Luke kept from falling out of his chair. She could not have said what he thought she did. "Excuse me? You want me to rid you of..."

"Yes."

Murder might have been an easier request. It wasn't as if he couldn't imagine taking Carolyn Rydell to bed. Hell, he'd fantasized about that. But this wasn't a request to be lovers or have an affair. This was a cold and clinical *rid me of an inconvenient virginity*. The severe way she was dressed suddenly made sense. She was conducting a business deal, not engaging in seduction.

He leaned further toward her and took one of her hands into both of his. It was cold, and he found himself rubbing his thumbs along her fingers to warm them. "Caro, I don't understand. You're a widow, and I assumed you had—well, I assumed there was nothing inconvenient to get rid of. And if this is not the case, then virginity should not be an inconvenience. It is something most women value." He tried to keep is voice low and measured.

Her chilled hand wrapped around one of his with a surprisingly strong grip. "My husband's nephew, Gerald, has found a doctor who will swear that Charles was impotent, and he plans to challenge the validity of our marriage on those grounds. And so I thought if I were ever asked to offer proof that

Charles and I had..."

"Wait! Kelton said lack of consummation would invalidate your marriage?"

Carolyn nodded, "He told me that he could take over the shipping company if Charles and I weren't legally married."

"Were you?" Luke felt her jerk away, but he continued to hold her hand tightly. He could see anger flash in her eyes, but the question needed to be asked.

"We were married at St. John's Cathedral in Calcutta. It was the standard Church of England service. Bishop Thomas Middleton officiated. Over three hundred people attended. There can be no question our marriage was legal. Gerald knows he can't refute that, but he's questioning whether ours was a true marriage for this, this other reason."

All Luke had to do was lie and tell Carolyn that her marriage could be questioned on the grounds of non-consummation, and he could have this fascinating woman in his bed. And Lord, how he wanted that to happen. His fingers tingled with the desire to discover if her skin were as silky as it appeared. He could easily imagine himself over her, in her.

But not like this. Not as a one-time business arrangement. That would be worse than never making love to Carolyn at all.

"Caro, Mrs. Rydell, I'm not a solicitor, but I'm

fairly certain that a marriage cannot be challenged for non-consummation. Kelton is trying to scare you. I have a friend who knows the law, or you can contact your own solicitor, but this needs to be checked before you take such a drastic step."

She suddenly looked more like a young girl than a businesswoman. "Could you talk with your friend without mentioning my name? I don't want to do anything that would cause gossip about Charles. He was a good man, and I wouldn't want to hurt his memory. This is the reason I couldn't ask the attorney that the shipping company keeps on retainer."

"Of course. I'll keep the question generic, but I think you have nothing to worry about."

Carolyn took a deep breath and relaxed back onto her chair, her hand slowly sliding from Luke's now loose grip. "Thank you."

He smiled, trying to feel buoyed by doing what was right and ignoring the part of him that wished he had done otherwise. "I told you I'd do whatever you needed—and in this case you needed nothing at all."

"Except your wise counsel."

"I hope it's wise. As I said, I think Kelton is just tormenting you. If this turns out to be the case, perhaps you can think of some way to pay him back for what he's threatened. If you need help with this, remember I am always at your disposal." Not that she'd necessarily need further help from him, not when she was surrounded by so many flower-bearing swains. "And now I need to leave so you can disappear before the arrival of your admiring horde."

She gave him a tremulous smile and stood when he did. He started to turn for the door when he felt her hand on his arm. Turning back, he was surprised when she went up on tiptoe and brushed her lips softly across his cheek. "You are a good man, Lucien Harlington," she whispered.

Her girlish kiss flashed like a lightning strike through his body. "I do have one question," he said. His voice was uncommonly husky. "Why did you ask me to do this and not one of the men who sent you flowers?" He didn't want to point out that with their gifts, these men had already taken the first step in what they obviously hoped was a dance leading to the bedroom. He tried to make the question sound like an afterthought. Luke didn't want her to realize how important the answer was to him. He hoped she had not chosen him because of his disreputable reputation. He would hate for her to have such a poor opinion of him.

"I like you," she said. "I feel comfortable with you. I thought if I surrendered my virginity to anyone, I'd be happiest if it were you."

Luke stopped by the drawing room door and gave Carolyn a smart bow. "Then I thank you, dear lady, for the almost honor."

After that, there was nothing else to say. But as he walked from Mrs. Rydell's house, Luke felt light of spirit. He smiled as he thought of how surprised society at large would be if they knew that he'd just done the right thing to his own loss. The shock would probably kill some of the *grandes dames* of the ton. It was a good thing his actions would always remain a secret.

Carolyn artfully spread the letters from the solicitor across the desktop. She wanted to make sure Gerald could see at least part of what was written on the papers, but she didn't want to make it too easy for him to read. The idea of his getting a cramp in his neck as he tried to take surreptitious peeks pleased her.

Lord Lucien's response to her needs had exceeded her expectations. Within twenty-four hours, he'd written that she had nothing to fear and had included comments from a solicitor that made reference to specific statutes. These latter pages were what she had strewn on her desk.

Gerald had quickly answered her note, so he was no doubt expecting some sort of capitulation. Most likely the reinstatement of the stipend she'd originally granted him. Carolyn smiled at the idea. That would never happen.

"Lord Kelton to see you," Perkins announced.

"Please show him in here," Caro said. She comfortably seated herself behind the desk and look up expectantly when Gerald entered. "Have a seat, Gerald." She waved a hand in the direction of the two chairs facing the desk. "This should take only a minute, but I thought it best if we met face-to-face to go over the problem you brought to my attention when we last spoke."

Gerald smirked as he crossed the room and sat down. Carolyn had thought his threat was intended to frighten her, but it was possible that the man truly believed he had the upper hand. His expression seemed to indicate this was the case.

"I've spoken with my solicitor," she said without preamble, "and have been assured that there is no reason that my marriage to your uncle could be invalidated." She tapped her finger on the papers on the desk to draw attention to them.

"That's absurd! We both know Uncle Charles was impotent." He reached to turn one of the papers on the desk in his direction. Caro placed a hand on the page and pulled it toward her instead.

"I've also been informed that if your repeating this gossip is seen to have a negative effect on the contracts Rydell Shipping has with the government, I could sue you for malicious slander. With the failures of so many banks in the recent panic, the courts are anxious to limit the areas of commerce with difficulties, and they wouldn't want to call into question the ownership of one of the larger shipping companies. I see no possibility your lawsuit would prevail. So your wisest move would be to keep quiet and act like I'm a well-loved aunt."

With satisfaction, Carolyn watched the blood surge into Gerald's face. She shouldn't take such delight in angering him, but it seemed only fair after he'd spent the last year making life difficult for her.

"You will certainly never be my well-loved aunt. I will scream that from the rooftops, and there's not a thing you can do about it. And as to this other—I think you'll discover your information is in error."

Carolyn had conducted enough negotiations to recognize bluster when she saw it. Her lips tipped up into a smile of satisfaction. "You never even checked the legal basis for what you threatened, did you? If you had, you would know that there is no way to void my marriage and no way you will ever get your hands on Rydell Shipping. The most you can do is try to blacken my name in society, and by now, you should have guessed that I'm indifferent about what others think."

"That much is obvious." Gerald's face had gone from red to the most amazing shade of purple. "I heard you were flaunting yourself at Hazelton's ball."

"I'm sorry you weren't there, Gerald. We could have danced." She gave him an insincere smile.

Gerald looked like he might have an apoplectic attack. Carolyn couldn't find it in her to feel badly if that were to happen. She was sure she was a much nicer person before she came to England.

"I doubt there was any room left after all the men who think you'll be their mistress had signed your dance card. Tell me, do all these men know that spot has already been taken by Lucien Harington?"

She must have shown some reaction, since the satisfied smile again appeared on Gerald's face. "What? Did you think I wouldn't know when that rake visits you? You were closeted alone with him yesterday for over half an hour.

Laughter bubbled out. "Gerald, you really need to decide if I'm your uncle's virgin widow or if I'm a morally loose woman with a string of lovers. I obviously can't be both—and if you were to suggest as much to others, you will only confirm that you are a fool."

He looked shocked that she had seen his arguments as illogical. "You're the one who is a fool," he said, standing abruptly. "You shouldn't have control of my uncle's legacy, and I'll eventually prove it."

Gerald stormed out, imperiously calling for his cane in the foyer. Caro relaxed and took a deep breath. She was confident that the man would continue to be an irritant, but she'd decided his threats were toothless. The worst he could do was to blacken her name in society, and, as she'd told him, she really didn't care what a group of useless, effete people thought of her.

But she did want friends. She was tired of a solitary life. She wished some of the businessmen she'd met had interesting wives, but the few she'd come into contact with were absorbed in their homes and children and had nothing in common with her. Any such relationship would be forced, at best.

Of all the people she knew, she could imagine a friendship with only one person—Lucien Harlington. Of course, offering the man her virginity was a rather awkward way to begin a friendship. But he'd not leaped at the chance to bed her, so perhaps friendship was possible.

She firmly believed that she wouldn't know until she tried, however, and her curiosity spurred her to try. She pulled a sheet of her stationary toward her and began composing a friendly invitation to dinner.

Intrigued—that was the word. Luke was definitely intrigued. It had been a long time since he'd been so pleased to receive a dinner invitation. Accepting it had been worth all Tremaine's teasing about finding a cache of money in unexpected places. Luke had given up trying to convince his friend that Carolyn Rydell was something very different than a purse he was considering marrying.

Exactly *what* she was remained to be seen. But he was going to pursue the possibility.

When he arrived for dinner, therefore, he didn't know exactly what to expect from the evening. Mrs. Rydell had expressed the need for a kind friend, and if that was all she needed, he would fill that place in her life. He regretted disabusing her of the notion that she had need of a lover, but being a friend was better than being nothing.

When he was shown into the drawing room, she dazzled him, wearing a rose silk dress that hugged her curves lovingly and made him glad for the return of the natural waistline in woman's gowns. She'd eschewed an elaborate hairstyle in favor of a soft arrangement that seemed held in place by a single comb. His fingers itched to pull that comb free and watch the shining darkness cascade down her back.

He tried not to be effected by her beauty. He was not completely successful.

"I'm so glad you accepted my invitation," she said, coming toward him with both hands extended. Luke grasped them, surprised anew by how normal holding her hands felt. "I'm sure you had many other entertainments to choose from."

"There's nowhere I'd rather be." His words rang with sincerity, since they were true. He felt layers of concern sloughed off him when he was in her presence, as if the care she'd given him while he was injured continued unabated.

Caro—no, he must think of her as Mrs. Rydell—gave a rueful smile. "I've been led to believe that you're a man-about-town, so you can hardly find a simple dinner exciting."

"With you it is. And I hope you do not believe everything you've heard about me, although some of the gossip is, unfortunately, well earned. I was unjustly accused of heinous behavior and when no one would accept my innocence, I decided to live down to others' expectations." That was a succinct and emotionless rendition of his situation, but he now realized he wanted Carolyn Rydell to believe his innocence without question.

"That sounds like a long tale best told over good food," she said. "Shall we go in to dinner?"

She led him to a dining room where two places had been set at a smaller round table by a large window rather than at the long, stately table in the middle of the room. In the fading twilight, Luke could see that the window overlooked a surprisingly spacious garden, more natural in appearance than carefully pruned.

"The rhododendron are in full bloom," Mrs. Rydell said, noting the direction of his gaze. "I was delighted to discover that shrubs normally grown in the Himalayans do well here in England. I'm sorry the light is fading and you can't fully appreciate their display. I often breakfast here and enjoy the view."

Luke had a vivid image of Carolyn Rydell sitting here in lonely splendor, flowers her only companions. The thought made him sad. "Do you miss India?" he asked.

"Oh, yes. But like the rhododendron, I'm confident I can flourish in this clime."

He could hardly refute that statement, so the conversational topic changed to the difference between the two countries, and the meal passed in companionable discussion. Luke enjoyed watching the candlelight flash in her dark eyes. He was fascinated by the way her skin picked up the shimmering light and seemed to glow. He wanted to run his hands over her exposed shoulders and see if they were as soft and warm as they appeared. The desire to taste her lips beat through him.

But Luke acted on none of these impulses. Carolyn Rydell had asked for his friendship, and that was what he would give her. He tried to pretend he was having a convivial meal with Tremaine instead of a woman who heated his blood. He had not imagined this pretense would be so difficult, however.

When dessert arrived, he didn't know whether to greet it with relief or disappointment.

"This is the only Indian component of the meal," she said. "I hope you like it."

Luke took a bite of what appeared to be a cool rice pudding. The sweet and nutty taste surprised him. "Very good. What's it called?"

"Kheer. It's one of the few Indian dishes my cook can manage without changing it into something more English, and, therefore, not quite right. When I find I can no longer stand a bland diet, my manager Sanjeet, my maid Amala, and I invade the kitchen and cook a traditional meal. Cook is horrified, but then the recipes aren't butchered."

"You can cook?"

His expression must have reflected his doubt. She laughed. "Of course I can. I was always surprised that my fully English counterparts in India seemed to be willing to starve rather than learn the rudiments of cooking. Even my own father told me that a lady needed only to go over the menus, not actually be able to prepare them, but this seemed such a boring experience."

"Do you find that most of the English ladies you've met are boring?"

"Not boring so much as purposeless."

Luke heard implied criticism in those words. He suspected she also viewed his entire life as purposeless—and in this, she was not off the mark. "Alas, the same can be applied to many people of both sexes in the ton. We're the product of the prejudices of our class, which sees actual work as something beneath us. Foolish, I know, but that's how we've been taught to look at the world."

She gave him an apologetic smile. "My late

husband's nephew, Lord Kelton, has made this prejudice very clear. My being in trade is probably my second greatest sin in his eyes."

"And what's the greatest?"

"Not giving him money made from that trade." She laughed, and Luke joined her. Viewed from her perspective, the whole lot of those who clung to shabby gentility rather than work did look like fools.

"I wasn't always without purpose," he said. "As a peer's third son, I was supposed to make my own way in the world. The three most acceptable routes are politics, the military, or the church. I couldn't see myself making speeches in Commons, and I was always more scholarly than martial. When the war against Napoleon ended while I was still at university, the church seemed the logical choice."

"You? A country parson?" Disbelief was written on her face.

While understandable, her skepticism hurt. He wanted Carolyn Rydell to think better of him. He smiled to deflect the sting. "I actually saw myself more as the Archbishop of Canterbury—but I acknowledge that I couldn't have started there. And I would have been happy with a parish in the country. I'm not all that enamored by London. I actually enjoy the slower pace of village life."

"Then, why are you in London?"

That was a question he'd asked himself more than once. "I have friends here. Activities." Those didn't equate to purpose, but it was the best he could do. The small stud farm he'd briefly imagined glimmered—and then was gone.

"What happened to the idea of your entering the church?"

Luke was glad that she wasn't laughing at the idea. "That opportunity was long ago," he said. "I mentioned earlier that my life had taken some unexpected turns that have led me to the here and now. I loved my studies at the university. If I was perhaps more interested in the intellectual side of religion, I would have still made a good minister, but I was accused of something so horrible that I was no longer an acceptable candidate."

And then he told her about Belinda Fuquay's accusations and his response. He didn't make excuses; he just gave her the facts of that terrible period of his life when all doors shut and no new ones opened. He spoke with honesty and regret. "I should have married her," he concluded, "but I imagined the real father would step forward. I had no idea she would do what she did."

Carolyn reached over and gave the hand lying on the table a quick squeeze. Until she'd touched him, he had no idea he'd clinched it into a fist. Warmth stole through him, relaxing taut muscles. "Why do you think she targeted you?" she asked.

"I've pondered that since it happened and have never arrived at a satisfactory explanation. I truly knew her only in passing. Maybe she thought I'd marry her for her dowry. In the end, I'll never know." He turned his hand over and grasped hers. His spirits were buoyed by her belief that his version of the situation was true. If only he'd had the same support from his family.

"I should be going," he said abruptly. If he stayed much longer he couldn't resist the urge to gather her into his arms. He hadn't felt this comfortable with anyone in years and didn't want to destroy their growing closeness.

"You'll come again?"

How could she doubt it? "If I'm invited," he said.

"You will be."

The warmth of her dazzling smile carried him out into the street.

Patterns for June 1825

CARO WAITED IMPATIENTLY FOR SANJEET to finish reviewing the documents that examined the feasibility of importing wine from Madeira. She could see his dark head bent over the papers through the door to the outer office. As he methodically turned the pages and made notes, she nudged the cut glass oil lamp and two paperweights on her desk into a slightly different configuration. She realized she was fidgeting but could do nothing about it.

When he finally finished and stood, she pretended to be engrossed in an unread shipping schedule.

"It's a workable plan," he said, entering her office. "I know this isn't your work, so who came up with this idea?"

"A friend. I thought it looked good, but I wanted to have your unbiased opinion." She hoped she didn't look too delighted with Sanjeet's evaluation.

He grinned as if he weren't fooled by her attempt to suppress her excitement. "Once the new East Indiaman is in service, short hauls to places like Madeira would put one of the smaller ships to good use. Especially if the projected sales figures are correct. But the potential market seems to have been carefully researched and the sale of fortified wine appears to be steadily growing. I assume you will want to pursue this."

"Yes. It would make sense to have contracts in place before the new ship is finished. Assuming the shipbuilder meets the anticipated dates—"

"Perhaps a big assumption." Sanjeet raised his eyebrows and gave her an apologetic smile. He'd recently been spending a lot of time at the Blackwall Yard, coaxing the shipbuilder into staying on schedule.

Caro smiled back. "I've no doubt your persistence will ensure that *Rydell's Pride* will launch very close to when expected. If that's the case, *Fancy's Flight* should be available to try this shorter run."

"Do you want me to begin working on this?"

"Not immediately. I thought I'd see if the friend who had the idea wanted to be involved."

Caro could tell that Sanjeet wanted to quiz her about this mysterious "friend," but he wisely chose to forego that line of inquiry and returned to his own work. She wished she too could get something done, but her mind was now firmly fixed on her friend—for Luke had indeed proved to be one.

And that was the problem.

Over the past month, she'd come to want something more than friendship from him. But Luke had dutifully stuck to the role she'd assigned, restricting physical contact to a brief brush of his lips across her forehead when he left her house after dinner. At least they'd progressed to meeting for dinner twice a week and the intimacy of using first names, but she wanted more—and wasn't sure how to get it.

She'd attempted seduction last week by wearing a sari to dinner. Her late husband Charles had told her the consensus of the men at the English clubs in Calcutta was that there was nothing more exotic and alluring than a woman in Indian dress. This must have been the opinion of only men on the Indian subcontinent, however, since wearing a sari seemed to have no effect on Luke at all. If anything, he was more meticulously proper than ever.

Of course, this was the same evening that he'd arrived with his idea of importing Madeira. His extensive research confirmed that the market for the wine was expanding and that of all vintages, Madeira was the most consistent and undamaged by transport. Luke had presented his written report like the gift she took it to be. His enthusiasm about his findings was contagious, and she'd forgotten to be seductive in her own delight with the scheme.

When she thought it was a legal necessity, she'd asked him outright to be her lover. Perhaps that was the best way to handle the situation. But fear of rejection kept her silent. He'd be coming again for dinner in two nights, and she needed to come to some sort of decision.

She worried the problem like a loose tooth. With chagrin, she realized finding a solution to this was more important to her than where and when her ships were sailing.

Luke lounged against a column at the edge of the ballroom and watched the swirl of color around him. He didn't look for Caro, since he knew she wasn't attending this ball. He wouldn't be here himself except he'd promised Tremaine he'd distract Sir Reginald Cleary when asked. Luke had no idea what Tremaine was up to, but the man did love to secretly skulk around. Since Luke had made use of this ability, even if it hadn't been fruitful, he couldn't refuse to help Tremaine in return when asked.

The orchestra began a new set—a waltz. Lord, he wished he'd convinced Carolyn that she should come. He'd dearly love to glide around the room with her in his arms. But she was adamant about staying out of the public's eye. He hoped this wasn't an indication she didn't want her name attached to his in any way.

Their time together had fallen into a pattern over the past month. He'd initially gone to dinner at her house once a week, but that had now expanded to twice. They'd also progressed to where he now anticipated a goodnight kiss. He wanted more, of course, but had not pressed her. She continued to want only friendship and, even if it took all his self-control, he'd give her friendship.

Last week, however, he'd been hard pressed to ignore his raging lust. He'd arrived to find her dressed in an all-too-tempting red sari. The gold threads in the diaphanous material had caught the candlelight, and she'd shimmered like a flame. Even though the style was flowing, the sari had lovingly highlighted each of her delectable curves and illustrated how alluring and supple the female body could be when not encased in a corset.

He'd wanted to pull her into an embrace and explore every inch of her tantalizing body. When he'd glimpsed her bare feet, one slender ankle encircled by a gold band, he'd nearly come undone. He'd been thankful he'd arrived with some notes on suggested imports. It gave him something else to think about. But it had been hard. Actually, he'd been hard, and he hadn't wanted to scare Carolyn away with the knowledge of his reaction.

Lord, he was becoming aroused just thinking about how she'd looked. He forced his attention back to the twirling dancers, but even the most arresting of the beautiful women waltzing around the room looked bland by comparison.

"I'm surprised to see you here."

At the sound of the familiar, bored drawl, Luke pasted a pleasant smile on his face and turned to greet the younger of his two half-brothers. David was eleven years Luke's senior, and the two men had long ago decided they had little to say to one another. Whereas their eldest brother, Templeton, was truly humorless and rigid, David's propriety was assumed. David indulged in debaucheries that Luke could only imagine, but David's pretense of moral rectitude had fooled most of the ton.

Tonight, his wife Patience accompanied him. If there was ever a woman more aptly named, Luke had not met her. Patience had to exemplify that virtue to put up with her philandering husband, whose primary goal seemed to be to spend her inheritance as quickly as he could.

"David. Patience. I hadn't thought to see you here either." His words trailed off as all his thoughts scattered. His breath caught in his throat as his attention fixed on the necklace draped around Patience's neck. A thick gold chain supported a large, pear-shaped yellow diamond surrounded by smaller clear stones.

He'd never before seen the necklace, but the canary diamond was very familiar. He distinctly remembered his mother pouring the brilliant stones from a leather bag onto her bedspread. He saw his own childish hands arranging the sparkling gems into a pyramid shape topped by the big, yellow diamond. The cut, the color, was firmly etched in his mind. No wonder Tremaine hadn't found the jewels in Templeton's safe. David had had them all along.

"You're in good looks tonight, Patience," Luke forced out. "Is that a new necklace? It's lovely."

Patience flushed with pleasure. She was a retiring, plain woman, but anyone would have sparkled wearing such a gem. "Thank you, Lord Lucien. My husband recently gave me this wonderful necklace for our anniversary." She beamed up at David. "I'm afraid his valet spoiled his surprise a bit, however, when he found the package in his coat and gave it to me."

"David has always been thoughtful." Luke was amazed he could utter such a lie with a straight face. He wondered if the valet who'd handed the packet to Patience was still in David's employ. He suspected the necklace had been intended for a different neck than the one it now adorned.

David's face continued to wear an artificial smile. He didn't seem concerned that Luke would recognize the stone. Most likely, David had no idea that Luke had ever seen the gems. But having seen this distinctive one, Luke now knew who had the jewels. Jewels he would retrieve—as soon as he and Tremaine could figure out where they were kept.

As if conjured by his thoughts, Tremaine appeared next to him. "You're needed in the card room as a fourth," his friend said, slapping him on the back in overdone bonhomie.

"Oh, right." Luke pulled his gaze away from the necklace, but not before Tremaine had noticed where Luke's attention lay and had taken his own quick glance. With a brief mumble of pleasantries, the two men moved toward the card room.

"The big canary diamond?" Tremaine asked.

"Yes, one of my mother's." Luke's voice shook with suppressed excitement. The possibilities he'd previously imagined again flooded his mind, only this time, the idea of a distant stud farm held less appeal. Now he saw himself investing in shipping enterprises. He'd long ago researched the value of loose gemstones similar to those he remembered, and if even the bulk of them were still available, he'd be on a solid financially footing. He would then no longer be an impoverished suitor and could offer Carolyn Rydell more than friendship.

Marriage!

The idea burned through him like the first drink of inferior brandy. How had he not known this was his true goal? Had he repressed the idea because he knew everyone would assume he was attracted primarily to her money? New vistas opened before him.

"I can feel your excitement," Tremaine said, "but for now you promised to divert Cleary's attention. It would be most unfortunate if Sir Reginald were to decide to return to his house for the next hour. Do you think you can keep him in a card game for that long?"

"If you'll help me retrieve my jewels, I'll keep the man there until the sun comes up."

"An hour will do," Tremaine said dryly. "And it's always been my dream to be part of a truly spectacular jewelry robbery. If that diamond was any indication, your haul will be spectacular."

Caro jolted awake. It took a few heartbeats to realize the sound that had roused her from sleep was the banging of her doorknocker. A summons in the night was never a good thing. Her mind began categorizing possible disasters as her body slid from her bed and she began searching for her robe in the dark.

Her hand had just touched the heavy satin of her wrapper when she heard Perkins answer the door.

Her butler would undoubtedly be armed. He was no fool. He knew danger often arrived in the dead of night. She was fortunate the female staff slept in a back wing, or she'd have a hysterical Amala on her hands. When Caro had been a child, Amala had often frightened her with tales of the horrors that lived in the dark. Caro suspected Amala believed every one.

Slipping on her robe, she paused as she opened her own door and listened to what transpired in the hall below. She heard a whispered conversation, with no indication of anger or concern. She silently moved out onto the upstairs landing.

"You should have known that at this time of night Mrs. Rydell would be abed," Perkins said. He was limned by the glow of the candle he carried but had only opened the door part way, so Caro was unable to see who stood there from her vantage point two stories above.

"I know. It was stupid of me. I was at a ball, and the hour didn't seem all that late." Luke's voice, she was sure of it.

"Most of us have jobs that require us to get up in the mornings." Perkins sounded dismissive, as if he were getting ready to close the door.

"I can only apologize again. Please have Mrs. Rydell contact me as soon as possible in the morning."

"I'll speak with Lord Lucien." Her voice rang out in the darkened foyer. Whatever had brought Luke to her door must be important, and since he was here and she was awake, there was no need to wait until morning.

Luke pushed past Perkins and came into the hall. In the faint light, the two men seemed to be glowering at each other.

"Don't attempt the stairs without light," Luke said simultaneously with Perkin's "I'll bring the candle."

Perkins rapidly came up the two flights to where Carolyn stood. "I'll light your way down to the drawing room," he said, "and Lord Lucien can see himself up."

Caro found it amusing that Perkins thought she needed light to go down one floor in a house she knew well, while Luke had been abandoned in the dark to make his way up one flight. Sometimes men, regardless of age and station, behaved like such, well, men. She noticed the tail of her butler's nightshirt hung down below his coat and the back of his hair stood up like a cockscomb. Since Perkins prided himself in his meticulous grooming, it was probably his dishabille as much as the lateness of the hour that caused his grumpiness.

She followed him down the stairs and waited while he lighted more candles in the drawing room. Luke had also entered and stood near the door until Perkins seemed satisfied with the brightness in the room.

"That's quite sufficient," Caro said. "You can return to your rest. I'll see Lord Lucien out when he leaves."

Perkins looked as if he might argue, then acquiesced and left.

"I fear I am no longer in your butler's good graces," Luke said.

Caro laughed. "No, I don't believe you are. But please be seated and tell me what has brought you here so late." Following her own advice, she took her normal seat in the wingback by the hearth. As she slid into the chair, the realization that she was entertaining in her nightclothes struck her. No wonder Perkins had been hesitant about leaving her alone.

By comparison, Luke wore his evening finery. Even his cravat still looked crisp. The man seemed unable to settle, however, and prowled the room like a hungry cat. He finally stopped behind the chair that matched her own, his hands clutching the top of the back as if to hold himself in place.

"I had the most amazing revelation this evening and couldn't wait to share it with you. I again apologize for the lateness of the hour. In my enthusiasm to see you, I really didn't consider the time." He looked down at where his fingers dug into the material of the chair back as if embarrassed, but when his eyes again returned to hers, his face glowed with a brilliant smile. "I want to marry you."

A myriad of emotions shot through her. Initially joy. The idea seemed so right. Uncertainty swiftly followed. Had his financial position suddenly worsened and he needed her money to bail him out of a tight spot? And lastly disbelief. No man of value would want to marry her for herself alone. She was well acquainted with the tons feelings about her mixed blood.

These thoughts tumbled over one another in a matter of seconds, leaving her confused as to how she felt about his statement. "Is this a proposal?" she asked, realizing the words sounded inane as they left her mouth.

"Yes, I suppose it is, although I suspect I'm going about it very poorly."

She felt herself grin at the absurdity of the situation. "I'd have to agree with your conclusion."

"Let me explain, then."

"That would seem a logical idea, but first, is there a reason you are hovering behind a chair rather than sitting in one?"

Luke glanced around, as if surprised at his location. "It seemed a good idea when I first came in and saw you all warm and tousled from your bed. I had this powerful compulsion to loosen the rest of your hair from your night braid and then undo that lovely robe to see if your nightgown is as prim as the bit sticking above the neck of your wrap would suggest. At which point, I'd probably fall on you like a ravening beast and manage to convince you that you wanted nothing to do with me. And so, I'm using this chair as a shield—which is ridiculous. Good Lord!"

Shaking his head, he came around the side of the chair and lowered himself into the seat. Caro felt a powerful compulsion of her own. She wanted to leap from her chair into his lap and discover just what happened when one was fallen upon by a ravening beast. It sounded quite arousing. She wondered how both of them could have taken leave of their senses simultaneously.

"Let me begin at the beginning, so my revelation makes sense," Luke said.

She nodded encouragement. Her scattered senses made any sort of logical comment impossible.

"My mother was my father's second wife. Well, you would have guessed that since I have older half-brothers." He shook his head again. "Mother and her family escaped France during the Terror. Like most émigrés, they brought their portable wealth with them. In my mother's case, this was a large quantity of gemstones. I remember playing with them when I was a young boy.

"As I grew older, I lost interest in pretty baubles, but Mother always mentioned them as my legacy. When the whole Lady Belinda disaster came about, however, I didn't see my mother for a few years—and then, only when she was dying. After her funeral, I asked my father about the stones, and he told me my mother had sold them to help other émigrés."

Carolyn sat transfixed. She couldn't see how lost jewels could lead to Luke's irrational desire to marry someone his family would find unacceptable. Regardless of his present estrangement, this tale alone showed he still cared for them.

"I didn't believe him." Luke continued. "I'm not proud to admit that I even helped break into the family's most secure safe, with the idea of stealing back what should be mine. But the jewels were never found. I began to think my father was right and that there was no inheritance to help see me into a comfortable life."

He suddenly leaned forward, his eyes avid. "And then tonight, I saw my brother David's wife wearing one of the larger stones. Hopefully, the bulk of the jewels my mother intended for me are intact. David must have stolen them. My job now is to steal them back. At which point, I will no longer be the impoverished Lord Lucien." He gave her a blazing smile. "I'll be a worthwhile suitor of a wealthy widow."

In one smooth movement, he went down on one knee before her. "Carolyn Rydell, would you do me the great honor of being my wife?"

To have this startlingly handsome and good-hearted man all for herself for the rest of her life was a dream. "Yes" hovered on the edge of her lips. But dreams belonged to the land of sleep and wishful thinking—and she was awake.

She would never fit into Lord Lucien's world. She would always be the half-caste outsider. People would assume Luke had married her for her money, and if his illusive legacy didn't materialize, this would probably be the case. She doubted Luke would be happy with the title of Fortune Hunter forever tied to his name.

And if he did recover his lost fortune...he would be tied to a wife who would never be accepted by his peers. How long would it be before he found her an embarrassment, before everything good between them dissolved into something bad?

If she didn't care for him as she did, she might be willing to settle for a half-life, for a pretense of happily ever after. But she did care. She probably loved the man. And because of this, she would grasp the here and now, and not worry about some improbable future.

"No," she said, taking his hands in hers. "I will not marry you, but I'd very much like you to be my lover."

No? Luke couldn't believe Caro's answer.

No? After he'd explained that his prospects were greatly improved. After he'd come to her, heart in hand. Anger surged through him, and it took a moment for the second part of her statement to sink in.

"You're rejecting my offer of marriage but are willing to be my mistress?" He needed clarification for this bizarre situation.

"Yes." Her dark eyes were tear-filled. "But I prefer the word 'lover,' since mistress suggests a woman who is kept and I see this as a meeting of equals."

He rolled back onto his feet and moved away. Motion and distance seemed imperative. He was torn between the desire to either kiss her or throttle her. "It's nice you see us as equals." His voice was tight.

Caro stood and took a few steps toward him, her hands held out before her in supplication. "Luke, you're imagining some offense where there is none. Don't you see that I'm not rejecting you? I'm rejecting marriage—especially to someone I care about. I would be a millstone around your neck. My heritage will never change. I'll never be accepted by English society."

Luke shook his head in negation. He was certain Caro believed what she was saying. She'd told him that in India she'd been welcomed only in the merchant portion of Anglo-Indian society, and he could see how that exclusion had hurt her. But it wouldn't be like that here. He would see that it wasn't.

Caro frowned with intensity. "If you retrieve your legacy, you'll be able to marry a *real* lady, one with a sterling background who would be accepted by society and your family. If I were your wife, however, you would have to endure the subtle snubs and snide comments that I've become accustomed to. You'd eventually realize marrying me was a mistake and come to hate me."

"That's ridiculous—"

"Let me finish before you say things you'll regret." She overrode him, voice strident. "If you never find the gems, people will say that you were willing to overlook my heritage and the fact that I'm in trade to get your hands on my money. They will see you as venal and grasping—a joke. And you'll soon come to resent that, and you'll hate me.

"Don't you see that regardless of which scenario unfolds, you'll end up hating me? Is it not better that we have a glorious here-and-now than end up with recriminations and hate?

Luke searched for the words that could convince Carolyn that her assumptions were wrong. "I could never hate you, Caro. I love you—and you're the only woman I've ever said that to. I want to spend my life with you, not some stolen hours. My reputation is such that society at large will wonder how you lowered yourself to take my name. My friends, however, will happily get to know you and envy me for the lucky man I'll be."

Luke understood her reservations, but he wanted her to see that her concerns for him were of no account. He knew he wasn't much of a marital prize, but he would spend the rest of his life trying to make her happy. "We could have a good life, a full life. One filled with joy."

The tears that had been shining in her luminous eyes finally overflowed into twin trails down her cheeks. Something in him snapped, and he stepped forward, gathering her into his arms. At first she felt wooden. Then she slumped against him, her head resting on his chest just above his heart. He wanted to sooth her tears. He needed her in his arms always. Couldn't she feel that this is where she belonged? "I love you, Caro. Say you'll marry me."

She pushed back slightly until she could look up into his face. "And I love you, Luke. So, by definition, we are already lovers. I want you to make this a physical fact. I'm a twenty-nine-year-old widow and no one has ever made love to me. I want that person to be you—now, tonight. Don't ask me to make decisions about the future...just love me."

She loved him! She was warm and pliant in his arms. He was not made of stone. He lowered his mouth to hers. This was not the chaste, goodnight kiss they had previously shared. Her hands drifted up over his shoulders to grasp the nape of his neck.

With the slightest touch of his tongue on her lower lip, she relaxed her mouth, allowing his tongue to enter.

He could feel her initial surprise, reminding him of her lack of experience. He should proceed more slowly to avoid frightening her. Caro's whispered "just love me" called to him to make this experience one of exquisite delight.

He felt as if this time would be his first time. He was practiced at pleasuring women, but he'd never before truly made love. He found himself unsure for the first time since he was a boy. This would be a new experience for them both. He needed to remember to treat Caro with care.

But when she moaned low in her throat and responded to his deep kisses with untutored enthusiasm, he couldn't stop his hands from roaming over her body. His fingers slid across the satin of her robe, down her sides until they traced the lovely swell of her buttocks. He fought the urge to grip the tempting mounds and pull her tightly against his straining arousal. Instead, he moved his hands upwards until they cupped her unfettered breasts.

She arched her back, offering more access. He ran a line of feathery kisses along her jaw and the side of her neck as his hands stroked downward, seeking the tie to her wrapper. He wanted to strip both it and her maidenly nightgown from her lush body.

He stopped when he encountered the knot. No, this shouldn't happen here in the middle of the brightly lit drawing room. "Can we blow out all these bloody candles and go up to your room?" he asked, knowing if she were to reject him, this would be the time.

"Yes." The word was a sigh, a promise. Then she slipped from his arms and began circling the room, extinguishing the flames. Luke joined the task until only one candle burned on a table near the door.

Caro crossed the room and picked up the remaining light. She held out her hand. "Will you come with me upstairs?"

He slipped his fingers into hers. "Wherever you lead, I'll follow."

She gave a soft chuckle and pulled him toward the foyer.

Caro brazenly led her lover—or soon to be lover—up the stairs. She felt wanton, free. She could not, would not, feel ashamed of desiring this exceptional man. She felt she had always existed on the fringes of life and was now about to discover the center. She had been a long time coming to this place and time, but now that she was here, she would take full advantage of the opportunity.

Her confidence and buoyant spirit lasted until they reached her bedroom and the door had clicked shut behind them. Then nervousness and uncertainty assailed her. If rumor was to be believed, Luke's lovers were legion. What if he found her wanting? Heavens, how could he not? She had only gossip and temple carvings to guide her.

The candle in her hand weakly illuminated this, her private space. A room designed for comfort, not for beauty. She saw it as if through his eyes. The bed left in disarray from her sudden rising. The desk with its businesslike, neatly stacked papers. The chair draped with the plain workday dress she'd chosen for tomorrow. This was not a lady's boudoir set for seduction.

This was a mistake. She should tell him to leave. She was confident that even now, at this late juncture, Luke would do as she asked.

Before she could act, Luke gently removed the candlestick she clutched in her hand and placed it on a low table. She realized she'd stood frozen in the middle of the room for what? A minute? An hour?

He softly cupped her faced in his hands and lowered his mouth to cover hers with a whisper of a kiss. "It's all right, beloved," he said, as if he had recognized her discomfort.

She melted into the kiss, her arms sliding around his waist. Through his fine linen dress shirt she felt muscles tighten and shift under her hands.

His shirt? She pushed back in surprise. Behind Luke lay a trail of discarded clothing—jacket, waistcoat, even his shoes, left in an odd pigeon-toed configuration.

Following her glance, he shrugged and gave her a mischievous grin. "Yes, I hear the ghost of my nanny scolding, but what else could I do? You were so far ahead of me."

She chuckled and the uncertainty that had assaulted her disappeared. This was Luke, the man she loved and who loved her in return. Here was warmth and acceptance. She had nothing to fear. She wrapped her hands around the back of his neck and pulled his smiling mouth down to hers.

His tongue dueled with hers as his fingers made quick work of the knot holding her robe together. He kissed down the side of her throat as he slid the wrapper from her shoulders to pool at her feet. His hands moved from her arms to cup her breasts, teasing the peaks with his thumbs through the thin fabric of her nightgown.

She made a surprised mewing sound. Heat crept through her, concentrating low at the junction of her thighs. Her breath came in shallow pants. She leaned into his caress.

His hands moved, and she was suddenly swung off her feet and cradled next to his chest. In four long strides, he'd gently deposited her in the middle of her rumpled bed. He effortlessly followed to lie along one side.

"Your nightgown is as prim as I imaged," he said, nimble fingers already loosening the buttons at the neck. "Do you think we can dispense with it?"

Her first impulse was to clasp the garment to her, but the butterfly kisses he bestowed on the area of her chest he was exposing changed her mind. She wanted very much to be skin to skin with him.

"Only if you can quickly catch up." Her voice was surprisingly husky.

She'd just finished speaking when he stood at the side of the bed and pulled his shirt over his head. Her hand, which had been reaching for the bottom of her gown, stopped in mid-motion. She'd seen his chest when he was injured. Actually, she had seen all of him. But not like this.

This was a virile man, not one who was lying injured and feverish, and this made a huge difference. The candlelight shadowed his impressive musculature and highlighted the band of hair that ran from one flat nipple to the other and then arrowed down to where he was unfastening his fall.

He leaned down, stripping off his formal breeches, small clothes, and hose in one smooth motion. Caro admired his taut buttocks and powerful thighs. Then he turned back toward her and oh my goodness! She'd thought him impressive quiescent. Aroused, he looked like the Hindu temple sculptures she'd dismissed as impossible.

Her eyes surged back up to his face in shock. He was grinning. "You seem to have gotten way behind. Let me help you."

Then he was kneeling beside her on the bed. He gathered the bottom of her nightgown and lifted it. She shifted her rear off the bed enough for the fabric to clear, and he whisked it over her head. With a slight pressure on her shoulders, he eased her back flat. He knelt there, staring at her.

She would have felt embarrassed had his face not held a look of awe. "My God. You are the most beautiful thing I've ever seen."

Caro stretched her hands toward him, needing to feel him, skin to skin. He bent and kissed her lips, her eyes, her chin, and downward until he took her one sensitized breast into his warm mouth while fondling the other. She groaned and gripped his shoulders. The earlier heat she'd felt became molten and moisture pooled between her thighs. His hand moved down her stomach until he cupped the burning part of her. Unconsciously she splayed her legs and rose into his stroking hand.

A small, conscious part of her brain recognized this as desire. Desire she'd never before known. Glorious, soul-shattering desire. "Please," she murmured, wanting something, wanting more.

She had never imagined he'd replace his stroking hand with his mouth. Every muscle in her body tightened, her back arched, and her world shattered with a sharp cry.

He kissed his way up her body until he was lying over her, his torso supported by one of his corded arms, his arousal resting in the cradle of her legs. He entered her with one swift thrust. A quick pain and then a wondrous feeling of completion. Luke began to move and she followed his lead. The impossible tension built again, but she now knew what lay beyond the peak and strove for it. And then she was over, falling free. Crying her name, Luke joined her, collapsing to press her into the mattress.

He rolled to one side, pulling her with him until they lay tightly spooned together. He idly ran his hand up and down her side as their breathing returned to normal. "I love you," he said, "and I'm going to spend night after night showing you how much."

He gently kissed her temple and then to her surprise, rolled out of bed.

"What...?" She reached for him, not ready to relinquish the feeling of flesh-to-flesh.

"I have to go before your staff begins stirring." He was already leaning over to retrieve his strewn clothing. "Lovers by necessity must be discrete. Husbands stay, but lovers always leave before the sun and gossip finds them."

He dressed with amazing speed. All the while, she wanted to plead, "Stay! Stay!" But Luke was once again only following her dictates. This was the path she'd chosen. Tears filled her eyes, but she'd blinked them away before he returned to kiss her on the forehead, snuff the candle, and depart.

Then she let the tears come. They eventually became sobs, which finally evolved into whispered curses as pale dawn found its way around the edges of her drapes.

Changes in the Patterns for June 1825

"**Y**OU FOUND NOTHING?**" In frustration, Luke raked his fingers through his hair and slumped back in the threadbare chair in the sitting area of his rented rooms.

"There's no evidence of any jewels at your brother David's townhouse—well, except for the big diamond you've already seen, and you told us to leave that in place. We also checked at the house where David keeps his mistress. She has a few baubles, but they're nothing but paste. I imagine the poor girl thinks they're real, but my man says otherwise." Tremaine sprawled in a matching chair, booted feet casually crossed. He looked totally relaxed. Well, why wouldn't he be? His only motivation was curiosity, while to Luke, finding those gems meant everything.

"I've exhausted my ideas of where to look, "Luke said. "I guess we're through." Lord, he hated to say those words. The very thought that the gems were forever lost made him nauseous.

"Maybe at your father's..."

"No. My father is a self-righteous idiot, but I've never known him to be anything but scrupulously honest. If he said the gems had been sold to aid other émigrés, this is what he believed." The admission was difficult but probably true. His anger at his father for so easily believing the worst of him had colored his view of the situation. His father had often been overly stern, but he had never been unjust. If he'd had the stones, he would have handed them over to Luke, albeit grudgingly.

"Well, since we know David has at least one of the gems, there's every reason to think he knows where the rest of them are. We just have to ask him." Tremaine's smile was feral.

Luke uttered a filthy curse. "Yeah, we just ask him. I don't think there's much chance that we'll get an answer."

Tremaine hadn't moved at all, but something about him shifted from seeming like a cat asleep in the sun to one waiting patiently for a bird to land in striking distance. "There's asking—and then there's *asking*."

"As in...?" Luke raised one eyebrow quizzically.

"As in, I hire some muscle, and we snatch David and apply a bit of pressure until we get answers."

"Good Lord, Tremaine, David's a thief, but he *is* my brother. No one wants to know the truth more than I do, but we can't use torture to get it."

Tremaine laughed. "There's torture and then there's the threat of torture. Most people are afraid of the idea of pain more than the actual pain. All you have to do is make them think they will be hurt, and they'll disclose all but the most closely held secrets. Every time I've laid a razor against a man's privates, he's told me everything I wanted to know, and I've never nicked a one. Well, no worse that his valet might have done to his face."

Luke wondered if he really knew his friend. And perhaps more importantly, if he wanted to. "And just how many times have you held a razor, eh, there?"

"Four or five times. And I can guarantee that it has always worked."

"Heavens. I assumed you worked for king and country, but this sounds like you're a collector for an unscrupulous moneylender."

Tremaine straightened in his chair and shot Luke a look of disdain. "I did indeed do all sorts of questionable things for king and country. Most of it while you were a lad hiding from his tutor and stealing sweets from the kitchen. If I hadn't done those things, there's a good chance that you'd be speaking French as your native language. But since I'd learned the skills..." he suddenly shrugged and smiled. "What can I say? I get bored. I still do the occasional favor for Whitehall, but I also take private commissions. Case in point—I've been trying to help a friend find a hoard of jewels. Does that sound familiar?"

"Of course it does. And I appreciate your efforts. It's just that there seems to be a great distance between skulking around and pommeling someone."

Tremaine scowled at him as if he were a none-too-bright schoolboy. "First of all, what you refer to as 'skulking' most often involves breaking and entering, a much more dangerous activity that is guaranteed to get the blood flowing in one's veins. And I already told you, I never pommel anyone. I threaten—and that is usually all it takes.

"In your half-brother's case, I suspect it won't even take threats." Tremaine's smile was not pleasant. "He's always been a coward. I bet he'll fold the minute he's grabbed. Don't you want to get your hands on your legacy, or do you want to spend the rest of your life taking money from women like the pretty widow Rydell?"

Luke felt his hackles rise. He'd never taken a penny from Carolyn Rydell. He'd eaten her food, that was true, and they met at her house. But what else could he do? He could hardly bring her to his bachelor quarters. While the address was good enough, the interior bordered on shabby. No, he could never bring her here.

And he certainly couldn't expect her to marry him until he had a decent income and wasn't a pauper. The very idea of seeming to be a fortune hunter stuck in his craw. So, yes, if he were honest, he was willing to do anything to get his legacy back. Even if it included a tiny bit of judicious torture and pain.

"I'll go along with frightening the truth out of David," he said, wondering if Tremaine could tell this was an understatement.

"Good." Tremaine looked delighted. "Tomorrow night would be ideal. He always visits his mistress on Tuesdays and leaves around eleven. Your brother is—"

"—half."

"Your half-bother," Tremaine corrected, "is a creature of habit. I'll arrange for some bullyboys and an anonymous hack. We can meet here around nine and then wait outside his little love nest until he leaves."

"You want me to come with you?" Luke asked. Tremaine had previously rejected his help. He'd said Luke's inexperience would probably get them both caught.

"Of course. I think this is one time you need to be included. If you don't speak, he'll never know you're there. And this way, you can hear exactly what he has to say."

Luke felt his heartbeat speed up. Yes, this was something he definitely wanted to be part of. "I'll be ready at nine."

"Good. Wear old, dark clothing. Imagine you're going to clean out the stables and dress appropriately." Tremaine laughed. "It's my hope we get rid of a lot of shit tomorrow night."

He got up and clapped Luke on the shoulder. "I'll take my leave now. It's about time for you to visit your light-o-love and since you'll be missing your assignation tomorrow, you need to make the most of the time you have tonight."

Tremaine sauntered out the door. He was a slender, graying man who could easily be overlooked in a crowd. Tremaine was obviously someone who made a better friend than an enemy, and Luke was happy he counted as a friend. The fact that Tremaine not only knew David's schedule, but Luke's as well, was disconcerting, however.

Of course, his visits to Carolyn's house were hardly secret. He'd tried to be discrete, but there was little doubt that her staff knew what was going on. Perkins certainly did. If looks could kill, Luke would be dead. Obviously, the man thought Luke was taking advantage of Mrs. Rydell.

Luke hoped this wasn't the case. Lord, how he loved the woman. He wanted only her happiness—

and he truly thought being married to him could give her this. But only if he were in a financial position where people couldn't whisper that Caro had had to buy an aristocratic husband. As tarnished as his reputation was, he was still accepted by the ton, and foolishly, she was not.

If tomorrow night's mission changed his fortune, he would no longer take no for an answer to his proposal. He felt he was wearing down her concerns about her heritage. He smiled. The act of changing her mind was mutually enjoyable. Very enjoyable indeed.

Caro kissed the side of Luke's neck and ran her fingers through the soft, tawny hair on his chest. She loved the springy texture, which seemed as alive and full of energy as did Luke himself. She enjoyed these quiet times after passion had spent itself. She relished the closeness she felt during these relaxed moments. They gave her an opportunity for contemplation that the blinding delight of their lovemaking didn't afford.

"What are you thinking about?" Luke's sleepy voice came from above her head. "I can hear you thinking."

She pushed up on one elbow and looked down at his face. "You can't hear anyone thinking."

"I can hear you," he said with a grin. "You make this low hum, kind of like the sound of a light rain on the window. That's your thinking sound. You make other ones, of course. I'm particularly fond of the noise you make right before you come—"

She placed her hand over his mouth. "I don't need to hear a catalogue of my strange sounds."

"'Ere na ange." His lips vibrated under her fingers, and she laughingly moved them away.

"As I was trying to say," Luke continued, "I love the noises you make, and they're not strange. But when I hear the thinking sound, I know to pay attention. So, what's on your mind?"

"Nothing all that important. Just an irritant. Sanjeet told me today that Gerald, my slimy nephew-in-law, has shown up at the Blackwall Yards where our new ship is being built. He's been acting as if he has some control over Rydell Shipping and has made suggestions for changes that would add months to the completion, not to mention adding hundreds of pounds to the cost.

"Sanjeet has assured the shipyard manager that Gerald has nothing to do with the company, but it's hard for the manager to ignore someone with a title. Especially when the real contacts are an Indian and a woman."

"I thought Kelton had disappeared after you made it clear his threats about your marriage were useless. Of course, we have taken care of that 'inconvenient virginity' problem, should that ever come into question." Luke wiggled his eyebrows and grinned lasciviously.

She playfully gave some of his chest hairs a quick jerk. "Any villager in India could tell you that just because you can't see the cobra doesn't mean he's not lying in the deep grass waiting to strike. We only thwarted Gerald's plan to try to prove my wedding to his uncle was invalid. And beyond the matter of my virginity, I do need your help."

Luke was immediately serious. "What do you need?"

"I'd like you to go to the shipyard with Sanjeet tomorrow and introduce yourself as one of Rydell's principal investors—and then make it very plain that Lord Kelton has nothing to do with any of our projects."

He laughed. "What you want me to do is have Lord Lucien Harlington out-lord Lord Kelton, probably by mentioning my father the marquess a number of times. Do I have it right?"

Caro felt embarrassment heat her face. "Yes. I hate to ask you do to this. My word should be all that's needed, but that's not the world we live in."

She waited for Luke to see her words as an opportunity to again press her to marry him. As Lady Lucien, she would have more clout than plain Mrs. Rydell. To her surprise, he said nothing. Perhaps he'd become satisfied with just being her lover. Oddly, Caro wasn't sure if this made her feel better or worse. It was, after all, what she said she wanted.

Luke had been coming to her bed for over a week now—and it had been wondrous. She now wished he'd lied about a marriage not needing to be consummated to be valid. If he'd supported her misconception, they could have been enjoying this incredible relationship for much longer. Luke had awakened something within her she hadn't known existed, and she felt like a flower finally coming to bloom. Luke's presence filled in all the blank spaces inside her, holes in her life she hadn't even realized existed.

When it quickly became apparent that he would be visiting every night, the excuse of his coming to dinner had to be dropped. His coming twice weekly had already been noted and questioned by some of her gossiping neighbors. And so he now arrived well after the dinner hour, coming in through the tradesman's entrance at the back of the house. This way, his horse was hidden in the mews and he could use his own key without alerting her staff.

Not that the servants were fooled, but they were willing to pretend she'd suddenly developed a need for brandy and a cold collation to be left in her office. She wondered if she should have the drink and food delivered to her bedroom and eliminate the meeting in the office completely, but she felt that Luke enjoyed finding her there, supposedly working. Maybe he also thought the more neutral area would allow her to say no if she wanted.

At this juncture, she couldn't imagine wanting that. She could not get enough of him as it was. Acting on this thought, she dropped her head to follow the motion of her hand across his chest. When she came to one of his nipples, she swirled her tongue around its flat surface, watching in fascination as it tighten just as her own did.

Luke gave a low groan. She wondered if he realized he too made specific sounds at specific times. To check her hypothesis, she visited his other nipple and elicited the same noise. A giggle burst from her mouth. A giggle? Now that was a sound she would have sworn she never made. "You do realize you're making noises yourself?" she asked.

"Of course, but that was a don't-stop sound, so what are you doing stopping?"

Smiling, she again applied herself to discovering if he would make different sounds in response to different activities. He did. And then she did, since Luke quickly caught on to the game and began using hands and lips as well. They eventually ended in a tangle of sheets, sated and laughing.

When he slid away from her and began to dress, she felt tears gather behind her eyelids. This was the part she hated—when he kissed her on the forehead and repeated the litany that husbands stayed but lovers had to leave.

She realized this behavior was more effective than his asking her to marry him over and over. Because she did not want him to leave. Ever.

Tonight was different, however. After a soft kiss, he said, "Don't wait up for me tomorrow. I have something I need to take care of. If I am able to come by, it will be very late. I'll look for you here, warm in bed."

And then he was gone, leaving her feeling more alone than ever and cursing the circumstances that meant Luke would eventually be harmed if she married him.

"All this waiting is making me twitchy." For the hundredth time, Luke looked out the carriage window toward the townhouse where David kept his mistress.

"Waiting is what I do best," Tremaine said. He seemed languidly relaxed, although how this could be the case was beyond Luke.

For one thing, it was impossible to breathe within the confines of the carriage. Wherever had Tremaine found the thing? Submerged in the Thames? It smelled of damp and mold and something even less savory, although the latter might have been coming from the two large men sitting on the opposite seat.

Luke suspected that Tremaine did indeed plan to use torture. He was going to jam David's head into the armpit of one of his hired bullyboys, at which point David would confess to any crime, including high treason, just to get his nose away from the stench before he smothered.

"Ah, here he comes," Tremaine said. He nodded to the two ruffians, who exited the carriage with surprising stealth.

Luke craned his neck to try to watch the men, but they disappeared into the shadows of the surrounding buildings. David was an obvious target, strolling along the sidewalk, evidently on his way to a cabstand a block away.

Two dark shapes detached themselves from the gloom and hurled toward David, knocking him off his feet. There was a scuffle on the ground, then one of the big men stood up and draped an unconscious smaller form over his shoulder. In less than a minute Tremaine swung open the carriage door and the first of the thugs entered, dragging the limp body after him.

A large feed sack had been pulled over David's head. This extended to below his waist. Rope coiled around the sacking. This rope both held the material in place and secured David's arms against his torso. The first big man pulled David upright on the seat while the second entered the carriage and squeezed in next to David. The trussed-up figure was firmly lodged between two big men.

"I just tapped him," the first to enter said. "He should come to soon."

Tremaine nodded and rapped on the roof with his cane. The carriage jerked into motion. To make more room, one of the men put his arm over the back of the seat and grasped David by the opposite shoulder. The change in position increased the reek within the confined space. Luke hoped David regained consciousness quickly or he might never give them the information they sought. Instead, he would become a victim of murder by miasma.

They'd only traveled about four blocks when David started moaning. This was quickly followed by loud cursing and jerking about. Tremaine casually leaned forward and jabbed his cane into the chest of the shrouded figure. "If you want to get out of this alive, *mon ami*, you will sit very quietly and not make a sound except to answer my questions."

Luke hoped his mouth was not hanging open with shock. The voice he heard was nothing like Tremaine's. Instead, the words seemed to be uttered by a lisping Frenchman using schoolboy English.

"Say yes if you understand me," the French Tremaine said, pressing the tip of the cane with greater force.

"Yes."

"So, very good. Now would you be so kind as to tell us what you have done with the gemstones Lady Greyling intended for our use?"

The sack wavered back and forth, following the frantic motion of David's shaking head. "I don't know what you're talking about. I don't have any gems." His voice was high and breathless.

"Oh, it is so sad that you lie to us, no? Your pretty ladybird—she will miss your tupping."

Before David could make sense of what had been said, the big men grabbed his thighs, pulling them part and anchoring each leg under one of their massive ones. In the odd chance David had missed the intent, Tremaine reached out to unbutton his fall, saying, "Pierre, give me the razor."

Luke didn't know where he should look. If they were really going to bare David's privates, he had no desire to see them. They had been far enough apart in age that they had never seen who could pee further into the lake or, when they were older, who could get the first cock stand. Looking at his older half-brother's organ would be like looking at his father's.

Luke had never thought of himself as squeamish, but in this instance, he definitely was.

David relieved his quandary by blurting out, "I'll tell you. I'll tell you." before the first button was loosened.

"So, where are Lady Greyling's jewels?" Tremaine asked.

"Gone. Sold. But my step-mother hadn't intended the stones to go to anyone other than her son. I made up the story about their being given to French émigrés to cover the fact that they were gone. I made it up, truly. They were never supposed to be yours."

Gone. Sold. That quickly ended all Luke's hopes. At least he now knew. He slumped in the seat.

"And they were never supposed to be yours either," Tremaine growled. He grabbed the front of David's fall and gave a pull that lifted him off the seat and sent buttons popping.

"I know. I'm sorry." David screamed. "I was in debt to the moneylenders. I was sure if I had a stake, I could win enough money to pay the loans back. And even have enough to cover the worth of the jewels. I was going to give Lucien the money. I was. But I lost. I didn't have anything to give him. So I did the next best thing. I arranged for Lucien to marry an heiress."

Tremaine looked at Luke for clarification, but all Luke could do was shrug. He had no idea what David was talking about.

"And did this brother of yours marry this heiress? Did her money make up for what you'd stolen from him?" Tremaine asked.

High-pitched, hysterical laughter came from behind the hood. "No. He didn't. The damned fool threw it all away. I convinced Lady Belinda Fuquay, the most passionate and wonderful woman I ever knew, to name my brother Lucien as the father of our child. I couldn't marry her. I was already stuck with Patience."

His head moved from side to side, as if he were trying to see if his audience was sympathetic. "It wouldn't have been odd for me to spend time with my niece or nephew. I'd get to know my own child. My brother Lucien would have a wealthier and more accommodating wife than he could ever have hoped for. It was the perfect solution."

Luke couldn't believe that in the rapid tumble of words, he heard a note of pride. Pride? As if David thought he'd done something good. Did the man not mourn the loss of Lady Belinda? Of his unborn child? Could he not empathize with the hell he'd put Luke through?

"The bloodless vicar-to-be refused to marry her," David said with a chuckle. "Can you imagine?"

It was then that Luke hit him. He balled up his fist and aimed for where he thought David's nose should be. Gentleman Jackson's tutelage paid off. He felt cartilage break beneath his hand. And it felt good. Damned good. He decided to hit him again and again.

His mind blanked as his fists moved. He had no idea how long he would have continued, or how much time had already passed for that matter, when one of Tremaine's ruffians' fists connected with Luke's own jaw, knocking him back in his seat.

Tremaine was suddenly squatting in front of him, hands on his shoulders, pressing him back into the squabs. "Luke, what the hell are you doing. Are you trying to kill the man?"

Luke really had no idea. He knew he wanted to hurt David as he'd been hurt. "He took my life," he said. "Not just money. He. Took. My. Life. He stole my youth and my optimism. He ruined every hope I ever had. He alienated me from my parents. He made me a pariah to my peers. And you ask me if I want to kill him? No, I want him to suffer for all eternity. This 'bloodless vicar-to-be' wants him screaming in pain for the rest of his natural life. And I'd like that life of pain to be a very long one."

Tremaine shook his head and turned toward the other seat. The two ruffians had removed the sack from David, who slumped back against one of the big men. His nose sat at an odd angle. Blood flowed from it to mingle with that coming from his mouth and running down from cuts on his forehead.

Tremaine leaned over, sweeping his hands over the unconscious man. "I must say you've made a mess of him, but I don't think his injuries are fatal." Tremaine turned back to Luke. "I can understand your anger. It's certainly legitimate. So the question now is... what do you want to do with the son of a bitch?"

The rage drained out of Luke, leaving him exhausted and empty. He leaned forward, elbows on his knees, and tried to draw a deep breath in the fetid air. His hands hurt. Unsurprising, now he could see the damage that they'd done. He'd done. He flexed his knuckles, almost enjoying the pain.

What did he want to do with David? Luke wanted his half-brother to feel the loss and powerlessness that had dogged Luke's last few years. He wanted David to somehow give him back his peers' respect and his family's affection.

"I'd like to take David to our father's," Luke said.

Tremaine gave him a dubious look. "You want to barge into the Marquess of Greyling's townhouse in the small hours of the morning dragging along another of his sons, whom you've just beaten to a pulp. Do I have that right?"

"Yes."

"I'd advise against it."

Luke looked his friend directly in the face. "If you were me, you'd do it. You know you would. There's no time like the present for the old man to find out how wrong his assumptions about me and his precious David have been. And given the slightest opportunity, David will crawl away like the worm he is. Before he disappears and changes his story, I want this addressed tonight. Now."

Tremaine held his stare for a heartbeat and then nodded. "We need to let our muscular associates off first. I don't think they'd appreciate the notice of a marquess. And, to be honest, I'd just as soon stay in the coach. This is a family matter, and family matters are a quagmire I try never to walk through."

True to his word, Tremaine directed the carriage to Luke's family home. David regained consciousness before the two ruffians departed, but even after they had slipped away, he did nothing but whimper. Every time Luke looked in his direction, David cringed.

David seemed to have finally realized that the kind and compassionate man Luke had once been was irrevocably changed. The happy and optimistic vicar-to-be had been killed by lies and false gossip— and David had been the cause. Luke wanted David to be afraid of him and continued to stare at him.

As the carriage slowed, Tremaine captured Luke's attention by pressing a pistol into his hand. Luke was surprised to see that his friend had wrapped his cravat around the lower portion of his face so David couldn't identify him. "You may need this, monsieur," the French sounding Tremaine said. "I have found that butlers and footmen tend to resist late night visits to their master."

The weapon was uncomfortable in his hand. "Is it loaded?"

He couldn't see Tremaine's mouth, but a smile crinkled around his eyes. "*Mon ami*, there is never a need for an unloaded gun."

Luke nodded his understanding if not his agreement. The carriage came to a stop, and Luke reached across to take hold of David's arm. Tremaine pushed open the door with the comment, "If this scum gives you any trouble, shoot him in the *vulgaire*. He seems extremely fond of them."

From his reaction, it was obvious that David understood the instructions, and quickly exited the coach. He hadn't anticipated the carriage stairs would not be lowered, however, and fell to his knees. Luke jumped down after him, grabbed him by the collar, and hauled him, stumbling, up the stairs to the door.

Luke repeatedly banged the brass knocker with authority. This door had been closed to him for much too long. He was not returning as a repentant prodigal son. No, he was Azrael, the angel of retribution, and his time had come.

A sleepy footman cracked open the door. Without waiting for any conversation, Luke kicked the door fully open, knocking the footman back onto his rear. Luke strode in, dragging a whimpering David behind him. "Lord Lucien and Lord David are here to see their father, the Marquess of Greyling,"

Luke formally announced to the prone man. "Please tell him we will await him in the office."

As the man scrambled to his feet, Luke added, "If you think to return with help to evict us, please know that I will happily shoot sniveling David here. Just imagine how difficult it will be to clean up all the blood, brains, and other body parts splattered about. It will be much nicer if our father just meets us in the office...in say, less than ten minutes. If he takes longer, I'll leave. Bits and pieces of David will, of course, remain."

The footman scuttled away. Marching down the hall, Luke towed David in his wake. When they entered the office, Luke motioned his brother into one of the chairs surrounding the cold grate. Luke rested his buttocks on the edge of the desk.

"You know, I never liked this room," Luke said, looking around at the dark paneling and hunting prints. "Every time I was summoned here, I always received a dressing down. Well, maybe it's appropriate that we settle this here." He chuckled. "Although for now, its major advantage is its location on the ground floor. You don't look like you'd want to go up too many stairs in your condition." Luke smiled and waited for David to say something, but his brother remained mute.

Luke toyed with the pistol. He'd never liked guns of any sort and was surprised no one had thought to challenge him. He really doubted he could make himself shoot the thing. But there was something very seductive about the feeling of power that came from holding it.

He was casually swinging a foot back and forth, wondering if he were turning into Tremaine, when his father entered dressed in a hastily donned banyan. Noise in the hall suggested that others had come with him but wisely had not come in.

"Ah, here is Pater." Luke waved the gun in the general direction of the fireplace. "Have a seat across from David. He has a great deal to tell you."

The marquess looked with horror at David's battered and bruised face. "Good Lord, Lucien. Have you taken leave of your senses?"

"No. I think I've finally found them. But do sit down. My half-brother's tale takes a while. His excuses add so much length to the narrative."

His father gingerly lowered himself into the chair as if he thought any sudden movement would cause Luke to begin shooting.

"Okay, David. Please tell our father how you stole my legacy from my mother and then how you decided to make amends by marrying me to a wealthy lady who happened to be carrying your child."

Luke had anticipated having the threaten David. To his surprise, his half-brother began telling his story in a monotone voice. His eyes were fixed firmly on the carpet.

Watching his father was more interesting. As David spoke, his father began aging before his eyes. Color drained from his face. The hand he lifted to wipe his brow trembled. When David got to the part about Lady Belinda, he muttered, "Oh, my God," and looked at Luke with tears in his eyes.

The old Luke would have been touched by a show of sympathy from the man he'd worked so hard to please. The new Luke, buffeted by betrayal and deceit, felt nothing. Would this numbness last forever?

David's monologue finally ran down. The room descended into silence broken only by the swish of Luke's swinging leg.

"I am so sorry," his father said to Luke. "What do you want me to do?"

"About what? You can't give me my old life back. My character has been destroyed. I'll admit my behavior made my reputation worse, but at that point, I was trying very hard to live down to everyone's expectations."

Luke stood from his perch on the desk and began pacing, too agitated to remain in one place. "You cut me off from my mother, and no amount of regret can bring her back. The gemstones that might have given me the means to start over are gone. Oh, except for a large canary diamond I saw Patience wearing. Being married to David, I'm sure she earned it, but it's mine. I want it back. Other than that, I don't think there is anything you can do."

"About David, then?" his father asked. His face was so white as to be bloodless. "What do you suggest I do with him? I feel you have the right to have your say."

The right to have his say? Was his father a complete idiot? Did he think this would suddenly make everything right? The strange void in his emotions constrained his rage, but it was still there, beating itself against the bars of nothingness. And if his fury were loosed, it would want blood and mayhem and pain.

Luke smiled, but the effect must not have been reassuring, since his father winced. "As I see it, David is your problem. He's a self-confessed thief, adulterer, and liar. I could also name him murderer, for his actions caused Lady Belinda's death, as well as that of her unborn child. He also killed my own youthful hopes and dreams. What are the penalties for these crimes?"

The smile disappeared and he scowled at his father. "Of course, your problem in determining a just punishment is that you were complicit in most of David's actions. While you didn't steal my mother's jewels, when I asked you about them, you told me they had been given to French émigrés without determining of this were actually the case. At the time, you wanted nothing to do with me, since you'd also chosen to believe the lies David had spread. I suspect you were secretly glad that I was left with nothing. It was easy for you to wrap yourself in false righteousness and turn you back on your youngest son—a son who had always lived his life so you would find pride in his actions. If David killed my intended future, you were his collaborator."

Luke suddenly laughed without humor. "You ask what I want you to do? Be damned. For I truly want nothing else."

He looked at the shrunken, weeping old man and at the bloody slug that was his brother. And he felt nothing but disgust.

He walked from the room. The servants who had gathered just beyond the door silently opened a path for him through their numbers. As he left the house, he wondered if it had ever been his home.

He was pleasantly surprised to see Tremaine's odiferous carriage still sitting on the street. "Can I take you anywhere?" his friend called from the window.

He imagined Caro, waiting sleepy and warm in her bed—and he knew he could not go there. He was simultaneously too hollow and too filled with rage. He didn't want her to see the ugly person he'd become because of his family's betrayals. A creature with bloodied knuckles and a shriveled soul. He couldn't pollute her goodness and honor with his own blackness.

"I can't think of anywhere I want to go," he said.

The carriage door swung open. "Good. Get in. We'll get drunk together. That's what I do when I have nowhere to go."

"Do you often have no destination?" Luke asked, pulling himself into the carriage.

"Always, my friend. And I long ago discovered that even if I start out for one location, I will undoubtedly end up in another, so getting drunk is the best solution. Let's start at my club and work down from there."

Luke nodded. Getting drunk sounded like the best idea he'd heard today.

Patterns for July 1825

SANJEET KNOCKED ON HER DOOR but opened it without waiting for a reply. "A message, Memsahib. The runner is waiting for a reply." He motioned to the outside door located across the large outer office of Rydell Shipping. A ragged boy, nearly lost behind the tall clerks' desks, leaned against the doorjamb.

Sanjeet crossed to the desk and handed her the paper. The small man then shifted from foot to foot, as if unsure whether to retreat to give her privacy or to remain to give her support. He knew she'd been upset for these past two weeks and had undoubtedly guessed the reason. To forestall his having to make the decision to stay or leave, she immediately slit the seal and opened the note.

Would it be too late to hope for a dinner invitation for this evening? LH

No explanation. No apology. Her hand wanted to crumple the heavy paper into a ball and throw it across the room. Her heart wanted to take flight. She listened to her heart. Oh, she was a fool.

She pulled out a clean sheet of paper and wrote, *Eight then*, in her clear script, signing it *CR*. She folded the page with meticulous care and sealed it, part of her still tempted to sweep everything into the trash. Before she could act on that impulse, she handed the return message to Sanjeet. "Here's the reply."

He quietly exited, leaving her to stare at the original note. The first seven words seemed to express the real question—*Would it be too late to hope?*

Luke had disappeared from her life a fortnight ago. The night he said he might be late, she'd waited for him until nearly dawn. She'd planned to thank him for going to the shipyard. She wanted to make him laugh with Sanjeet's version of his overbearing lordly behavior.

But he did not come. Then or the next night—at which point, she was frantic, imagining all sorts of terrible fates. What if he were again floating in the Thames and she was not there to find him?

She finally sent a disgusted Perkins to Luke's lodgings, but her butler returned with the information that he was not at home. Not knowing whom else to contact, she'd written to his friend, Viscount Tremaine. At least Tremaine had answered, although she doubted his letter's truthfulness. He said Luke was involved in a family crisis and had been called out of town. He assured her Luke would contact her as soon as he was able.

And then, nothing. Just lonely silence as if Luke had never been—as if *they* had never been.

Slowly, concern coalesced into anger. Was she so unimportant that she could easily be dismissed from his mind? Amala read her distress and began again muttering about the dangerous habits of pye-dogs and how one should kick the curs and be done with them.

Eventually, her anger turned to pain. Why had he bothered to lie and tell her he loved her? She would have tumbled into bed without the need of a ruse.

But mostly, she missed him, the essential Luke, the man who listened to the problems of her day with understanding and could make her laugh when she least felt like it. Oddly, the loss of this closeness was more painful than the absence of the passion she'd come to enjoy. Memories of his body moving over hers haunted the hours when sleep would not come. But it was upon awakening that the hole in her life became most apparent.

Before meeting him, she'd learned to live with loneliness, but now loneliness had become a living beast with claws and fangs that raked her skin. Being with Luke had shown her how sterile her life had been. She feared returning to her solitary ways.

And now, after all this pain, he'd chosen to reappear.

Would it be too late to hope? She hated that she still hoped. Foolishly hoped. She knew there could be no permanence, eventually he would discover she didn't fit into his world, but she had hoped for more. More time. More closeness. Was it too late for both?

She'd always needed to know what lay on the far side of the hill, and so she could not let him disappear from her life without discovering the reasons for her sudden dismissal. While the knowledge might hurt, possessing it was better than not knowing.

But she could not, would not, let him know how devastating his disappearance had been. She would be calm and collected, the consummate hostess. She would look him in the eye and stare him down.

To do so, she needed to make preparations. Lord, yes, major preparations. A sumptuous dinner served by a beautifully dressed woman who was the epitome of indifference. She had so much to do before he arrived at eight.

Her feet crossed the room without her willing them to move. She opened her door and stuck out her head. "Sanjeet, order the carriage to come around. I need to go home."

"Yes, memsahib," he said.

Caro was crossing to retrieve her bonnet when it dawned on her that Sanjeet hadn't been surprised with her request. Instead, he'd given her a knowing smile.

Luke walked up to Carolyn's front door. He was done with sneaking in through the mews. He'd just finished reclaiming a large portion of his life. Now he was here to claim a bride. Unfortunately, he wasn't particularly confident about that outcome of this last endeavor.

At the door, Perkins was aloof but not overtly hostile. Luke hoped this boded well for his visit. This optimistic interpretation lasted the length of the hall but disappeared when he entered the dining room. The large central table had been set for two people, one at each end. Nearly twenty feet of pristine white linen separated the two places. Caro had made it very clear that the intimate dinners at the small table by the window were now relegated to the past.

Caro herself looked like a queen. She wore a cream-colored dinner dress that shimmered in the candlelight. Her midnight dark hair coiled elaborately around her head. Her chin tilted upward at a haughty angle. Her eyes were mysterious and unreadable. She was incredibly beautiful and completely unapproachable.

Luke had known his behavior would be hard to explain. He'd come prepared to grovel, if necessary. It now looked like he would not be offered the chance.

"Lord Lucien, please be seated," she said without preamble, being seated herself by a hovering footman.

Luke has no choice but to follow suit. From his end of the table, he had a view of a large silver epergne overflowing with flowers. From the far end, only the top of Caro's head and the puffs on her sleeves peeked around the massive arrangement.

A footman offered a choice of two types of soup. Luke chose something clear. If it had a distinct taste, he didn't notice. His mind was too busy planning ways to breach the physical and emotion distance that stretched out before him. Only the click of spoons on fine porcelain broke the silence.

Luke waited until he'd been served the next course and the footman had backed away to stand by the wall. Then he would wait no longer. "I much prefer a cold collation in your bedroom," he said in a carrying voice.

"My lord, we are not alone. I don't believe this is a suitable topic for conversation." Caro spoke more softly, but Luke could hear embarrassment lace her words. He wished he could see if he'd caused her color to rise. The more uncomfortable he could make her, the sooner she would dispense with this lunacy and actually talk to him. As plans went, this was not a particularly good one, but it was the only one he could devise.

"Don't mind the footmen, dear," he said. "I suspect everyone below stairs knows of my bedroom visits."

"Luke, stop!" She stood, her face appearing above the centerpiece like Venus rising from the waves. The closest footman made a grab for her chair, which was evidently in danger of toppling over. Her face neared the color of her dress. Luke realized she was more angry than embarrassed. But he also noticed he was now Luke rather than Lord Lucien.

"Why not ask the audience to leave? Then we can conclude our business in private and get on with enjoying what has every indication of being an excellent meal." Luke held his breath to see if she would follow his suggestion.

Caro looked at the attendant footmen. "Please leave," she said, to his relief. "I'll ring for the next course."

She sat down again, once more disappearing behind the blooms. This would certainly not do. He picked up his plate, silverware, and wine glass and strolled the length of the table to take the place to Caro's right.

"What do you think you're doing?" He noticed the defiant jut of her jaw. Yes, she was definitely acting queenly tonight.

"I'm getting close enough for a conversation and didn't want to let this excellent fish get cold." As if to prove his point, he took a bite. When she continued to sit and stare at him, he took a slow sip of wine, his eyes never leaving hers.

It was obvious that she was not going to speak and make it easy for him. Luke wasn't sure how to begin. She had every right to be angry. His behavior had been reprehensible. He knew he'd disappeared with no explanation, but how could he explain he couldn't see her while he'd felt he had a hole in his soul.

It was one thing to have your family falsely accuse you of wrongdoing. It was quite something else to discover someone in your family had set you up to take the blame for his own failings. He'd found the knowledge corrosive and had feared she wouldn't like the empty person he'd momentarily become.

He'd tried to hide in a bottle. He'd spent two days nearly insensate with drink as he wallowed in self-pity in his rented rooms. Then his eldest half-brother Templeton had arrived like Galahad on a white steed. Templeton, the biggest self-righteous prig he knew, squinting at Luke's unshaven face and demanding he pull himself together.

Had it been anyone other than Temp, he might have laughed in his face and continued on his destructive spiral. But too often in his life, Templeton had looked down his nose and found Luke wanting. So Luke had stiffened his spine and met his oldest sibling with anger. Somehow, in the loud and boisterous argument that followed, Temp had convinced him to let their father try to make amends. Temp made it sound as if Luke would be giving their father the gift of forgiveness, rather than their father giving Luke anything.

Who would have thought Temp could be so persuasive? Luke ended up cleaned and shaved and on his way to Greyling Hall, the family countryseat in Surrey, before he'd had time to think through his actions.

Perhaps Luke had enjoyed his father's groveling. Perhaps he felt that some reward was his due. He didn't think his actions showed much character, but the results were oh, so sweet. He was about to get everything he wanted from life—if only Caro would agree.

He took her hand. At first it was hard, wooden. But as he stroked his thumb softly across her knuckles, it relaxed. Now if he could find his own persuasive words to turn his possibilities into realities.

Caro could have held firm to her detached demeanor if Luke hadn't taken her hand and played his thumb along her knuckles. The sensation was so familiar and soothing, the flimsy wall she'd built around her heart weakened and eventually crumbled. His tale was equal parts fascinating and horrifying. She empathized with his hurt and anger at his betrayal by his half-brother David. She could understand how he could hold all of his family equally culpable. And she applauded his reaching a rapprochement with his father.

She was less understanding of his apparent desertion. But she had little experience with true despair. Sadness. Loneliness. Yes, she knew those well. She'd never felt the bleak nothingness that Luke described, however, and couldn't imagine how debilitating this could be. The pride that kept him from showing her what to him was ugliness—this she could comprehend.

But she had a sinking feeling that Luke had wanted to explain these things to her in person because they heralded the end of their affair. Deep inside, even if she refused to acknowledge it, she'd known he was too honorable and fair to leave without a word. This, she feared, was her notice.

"I initially resisted taking the money and the estate," Luke said. "I didn't want to feel like my complicity had been purchased. But my father and Temp convinced me that the cash and land were of no more value than the gems guaranteed to me through my mother's marriage settlement." He squeezed her hand and grinned like a boy. "So, you see before you a man of property."

"I'm delighted for you, Luke." She truly was, even if she did have to force the words out through a tight throat. She knew how much he hated lacking funds. And a country estate of his own was a long held dream he'd finally realized.

"The property is called Thorneby Hall. It's nothing palatial, just a manor house, but it's in good repair and the attached acreage is lush. Wonderful pasturage. Perfect for horses. And best of all, it's just a few hours from London. It will be easy to get back and forth on weekends and the like."

She could tell he wanted her to join his enthusiasm, but that was impossible. In her mind's eye, she could see Luke proudly riding over his new property, accompanied by some perfect, blond English rose. Bile filled her throat. She attempted a smile, but suspected it was more of a grimace.

Luke suddenly looked as unsettled as she felt. "Of course, some people will continue to believe I was involved with Lady Belinda. I'm sorry if that will make you feel uncomfortable. My family will put the word out that new evidence has come to light that exonerates me, but I can't point the finger at David.

None of us can. Involving him in my old scandal, no matter how deserved, would simply further blacken the family name—and involve his wife Patience, who has had enough to contend with over the years. She shouldn't suffer for his misdeeds."

"So David won't be held accountable for his theft or for destroying your name?" The words came out louder than she'd expected, but the injustice of the situation rankled. Caro didn't know David Harlington, but if they were ever to meet, she was quite sure she could denounce him for the thief and liar that he was. Luke deserved to have his name fully cleared.

Luke shook his head. "David isn't escaping penalty. It's just being handled within the family. He's been exiled to a family holding in Northern Scotland. It recently came to us through my grandfather's sister, and while we have a competent manager, no one goes there. It is a singularly bleak and lonely place, isolated from any type of society. Nothing but moors, wind and sheep. Father's pronouncement is that David can stay there until he rots. I suspect he'll eventually be allowed back, but I doubt that will happen any time soon."

Luke reached into his coat pocket, pulled out a large jewelry box and two folded papers, and laid them on the table. "David did return the one gem that he had not sold, which he'd had made into a quite spectacular necklace. It's the only thing I have of my mother's, and I want it to belong to my wife. I haven't changed my mind, Caro. I love you and I want you to be that wife."

She'd braced herself for goodbye. She'd been preparing herself for his departure with every word, telling herself that this was how it must be and that it was good they could part amicably. Luke had caught her completely unprepared. The wild joy that leaped up left her speechless. When she said nothing, he pushed the box and the papers toward her.

"Before you reject my suit, please look this over." He tapped his finger on the papers. "It's a proposed marriage settlement. It confirms that Rydell Shipping will always be your sole possession. You can run the company as you see fit. You can sell it or will it to whomever you choose. I'll have nothing to do with your company. I don't want you to think that I would ever take it from you."

Oddly, the idea of losing control of Rydell Shipping had never entered her mind. Why this logical conclusion had escaped her was unclear. When a woman married, everything that was hers automatically became her husband's unless other dispositions of property were explicitly spelled out in the marriage settlement. But for some reason, she had never feared that Luke would ever take what was hers.

He gave her a hopeful smile. "Of course, I hope you'd allow me to help you wherever possible. I must admit that I enjoyed the research on the sale of Madeira and I'd like to continue in a similar capacity. But the control will always be yours."

She didn't have to look at the papers to know that this was exactly what they said. Luke wanted her for herself alone. This realization bubbled through her like fast moving water over a shoal of rocks, frothing and shooting tendrils of delight into the air. Even Charles had married her to protect her, not because he wanted her above all others.

But she would not hurt Luke—and she felt that marriage to her might do so. "Luke, you've just been given the opportunity to redeem most of your former life. You should find a lady from your own class to love, to marry. You don't want to be stuck with a wife who is in trade. You don't want people snickering behind your back that you married a woman of questionable antecedents." Lord, the words were hard to say, but she needed to make him understand that regardless of their feelings for each other, she was unsuitable. She didn't want him to become a figure of ridicule.

He leaned forward and lowered his voice, as if conveying a secret. "Caro, I'll be marrying the Earl of Kelton's aunt by marriage, a lady to her fingertips, and a stunningly beautiful one at that. I'll be the envy of the ton. Your worries are groundless."

"I'm sure the Earl of Kelton will give me his ringing endorsement." She knew how hateful Charles' nephew could be.

Luke grinned with boyish delight again. "Actually, I think you'll find that your nephew-in-law will be offering to provide a wedding breakfast to show his support."

She didn't know whether to laugh or cuff him. "That will never happen."

"The wedding breakfast was my half-brother Templeton's idea. My father will be visiting Kelton tomorrow to suggest it—and believe me, Gerald Rydell doesn't stand of chance of gainsaying the Marquess of Greyling. Not unless he wants both himself and his mother frozen out of society. My father has spent a lifetime consolidating power and prestige. Kelton will not stand against him." Luke sounded confident of the outcome.

"Why would your father do this for me?" Shock raised her voice to a higher register. Such behavior by a marquess seemed impossible. The man had never met her. He was only taking Luke's word that she would be a worthy addition to the family.

He picked up her hand and began to place nibbling kisses on her palm. Heat radiated from the touch of his lips down to her toes, and all points in-between. "I told him that you were my happiness. That I couldn't imagine a satisfying life without you. In short, I told him the truth. So if you don't say yes,

I'll be forever unhappy and will look like an idiot to my entire family as I sink again into despair."

The glint in his eyes was far from despairing. He looked at her with both hunger and love. How could she say anything but yes—and so she did.

The minute "yes" fell from Caro's lips, Luke jumped up with a whoop, grabbed her from the chair, and began whirling her around the room. God, how he loved this woman. They made two complete twirling circuits of the table, laughing like children who had found hidden candy. They finally stopped by the sideboard, both gasping for breath.

"Need I say you have made me the happiest of men?" His words came out in staccato bursts.

"I know you've made me the happiest of women." Caro punctuated her comment by wrapping her hands around his nape and pulling his head down to hers. Her lips seemed to taste of laughter and happiness. He pulled her tightly against him. He relished the feel of her, a combination of strength and suppleness, like the steel used in the finest blades.

"How upset will your cook be if we don't eat what has every indication of being a feast?" he asked. As if preplanned, they both turned to look at the table where the excellent turbot with brown butter and shallots sat abandoned and cold.

"Aren't you hungry?" Caro's voice had a breathless quality that he suspected had nothing to do with their wild dance around the room.

"Starving. I haven't had the sustenance that I most need for a fortnight now." He placed his hands on either side of her beautiful, upturned face. He ran the pads of his fingers from the raven wings of her eyebrows along her temples to her shell-like ears, marveling at the satiny texture of her skin. Her dark eyes mirrored his own hunger.

In one fluid movement, he slipped an arm under her knees and lifted her into his arms. She gave a brief gasp of surprise, then twined her arms around his neck and nestled her head against his shoulder. He felt a flash of possessiveness. His! She was his forevermore, and he was never relinquishing her.

He pushed open the dining room door to find the dismissed footmen hovering in the hall. Their mouths gaped in shock. Further away, Perkins swung in their direction, his face a thundercloud of disapproval.

"She's agreed to marry me," Luke called out and made a quick turn on his heel, Caro's dress floating about them and probably showing an indecent amount of ankle and leg. Caro's laughter accompanied his maneuver. Perkins stopped in place, suddenly smiling. Her staff cared for her, and they would accept him as husband where they hadn't been pleased with his position as lover.

But the husband-to-be was still the lover tonight. He swept her up the stairs. Amala darted out of Caro's bedroom as they approached. Even she was smiling. How had the little woman known there was a change in his status? Word of an impending marriage could not have traveled through the house so fast. Perhaps it was some mystic eastern connection. Luke realized it was one of the few times he'd seen the little woman smile. It quite changed her face.

And then the door was shut on Amala and the rest of the world. Here, there was only Caro. And she was all that he would ever need.

He lowered her to the floor. The slide of her body over his was exquisite, and he again possessed her mouth. The velvet of tongues tangling together. The soft nibbles. The tiny gasps. Mine, his kiss proclaimed. Forever mine.

Without breaking the kiss, his hands rose to begin unraveling the glory that was her hair. Pins fell to the carpet with the sound of rain on new grass. And then the heavy weight of her tresses was released. He drew back slightly to watch his fingers stoke through the shimmering darkness. Night with stars, he thought, inhaling the spicy scent that rose from the thick mass. Night in a secret garden.

He turned her in his arms, brushing her hair over her shoulder so he could begin working on the fastenings down the back of her gown. His fingers trembled as they released each one. He'd undressed women, too many to consider. He'd even performed this service for Caro in the past. But he had never done so for his prospective bride. The emotion that now flowed through him shook him to the core.

When all her discarded finery puddled around her feet and she stood only in her shift, Caro turned and began unbuttoning Luke's waistcoat. He felt every movement of her delicate hands as if they were brands through the cloth to the skin beneath. He jerked his cravat loose and shrugged out of his jacket and waistcoat. He pulled his shirt over his head, and Caro was again there, kissing his chest and running fingers along the line of crisp hair that arrowed down to his trousers until they settled over the fullness there.

She pulled back to look at his chest, his face, his sandy blond hair. "You are the color of the sunrise," she said, the first words in this silent room.

"I hope I will always be your sunrise." Then he chuckled. "And your sunset and your midday. Any moment on the clock, I will be yours."

He lifted her effortlessly and carried her to the bed, pulling the shift from her as he laid her down. He watched her watch him as he stripped off the rest of his clothes. Her beauty caught his breath in his throat and as he came over her, a welling of tenderness brought tears to his eyes.

Their lovemaking was slow, each movement fraught with meaning, each sigh a song that had never before been sung. He marveled that all of the missteps of his life had somehow brought him here—the one place he was destined to be.

Only later, when Caro lay spooned against his body, did words seem possible. "I'll get a special license so we can wed whenever we desire. I'd be happy with tomorrow, but we don't want this to look rushed. I guess it will depend on when Kelton feels he can host our wedding breakfast."

Caro giggled, a surprising sound he'd seldom heard. "You are rather naughty to press Gerald to do this. I would imagine he will choke on the food he serves."

"The show of his support as well as my family's will do much to ease our way, and those of our children, into society."

She turned toward him. "How many of those children are you imagining?"

"Legions. Or however many their mother wants."

"I'm not sure about legions," she said, kissing him, "but right now their possible mother certainly wants." And then she showed him exactly what she meant.

Carolyn stood motionless at the window of her ground floor study and watched darkness creep across the garden, dimming the brightness of the summer flowers to gray. How long had she stood here woolgathering? She smiled. Her impending marriage was making her as moony as a girl in her first season.

She closed the curtains and turned up the Argand lamp on her desk. The light spilled across the packet Patience, David's now estranged wife, had left for her approval. Patience had made detailed sketches of the proposed bouquets to be placed in the drawing room for Caro's wedding. Caro personally thought all this fuss was a bit silly, but it seemed to please Patience, and she'd quickly come to like the quiet woman who had seemed to bloom with her husband's departure.

Luke seemed to think that being involved in the start of a happy marriage gave Patience a more positive view of the institution. He believed it was good for her to see that not all marriages were based on indifference and deceit, as hers had doubtlessly been. In consideration of Patience's feelings, for her wedding, Caro wouldn't be wearing the canary diamond that had belonged to Luke's mother. It had been Patience's such a short time ago.

Caro sat at her desk and began looking over the drawings. Her preference would have been for a collection of bright blooms, but Patience had chosen white flowers. Iceberg roses, hydrangea, and white lilacs glowed amid lush greenery. Patience was a talented artist. Caro smiled. She still favored reds and yellows, but this would be one of her many concessions to being more English.

Four more days. Only four more days. If time would hurry, she didn't care if there were any flowers at all.

A soft noise on the servants' stairs heralded Luke's earlier-than-usual arrival. He'd insisted on returning to his nightly arrival and departure via the mews entrance, although she was sure no one in the entire town was fooled, but he said he wanted her to be the blushing bride. Silly man. How she loved him.

She turned toward the door and her bright smile of welcome froze. Her nephew-in-law Gerald stood there.

"I guess I'm not who you were expecting," he said with an artificial smile. "I left Lord Lucien being feted by a few friends at Brook's and decided this would be a good time for us to have a quiet discussion."

"I have nothing to say to you. I have no idea how you got in here, but please leave before I ring for a footman." She'd often been irritated by, but never afraid of, Gerald. But something about him tonight raised the fine hairs on the back of her neck. His gaze seemed oddly unfocused.

He sauntered into the room like a man at his ease. "I thought we needed to discuss some details about this breakfast your intended's family has pressured me into having. I want to make sure it's exactly what you want. I have no desire to commit social suicide by angering the Harlington clan."

His request would have been reasonable had he called during normal hours, but there was something off about his being here now. As he advanced, Caro's impulse was to leap up and back away. But she'd be damned if she let him cow her. "I think you should come back tomorrow to discuss this," she said.

He sprinted toward her, faster than she could have anticipated. She rose from her chair, unsure of whether she planned to shout at him to leave or simply to scream. The opportunity to do either disappeared when he bowled into her, knocking her back into the desk. Before she could take a breath to alert the household, he clamped his hand firmly over her mouth. His weight bowed her body, pressing her shoulders onto the desk.

She squirmed and bucked against him, but she'd landed at an odd angle. One of her arms was trapped under her body and her feet couldn't get a good purchase on the floor. She flopped ineffectually, attempting to bring the unencumbered arm high enough to reach his restraining hand or to scratch his face. She tried to shake his hand loose, but his hold was firm and punishing. She wanted to bite him, but he held her jaw tightly closed.

Gerald steadied her body under his and reached up with his free hand to pinch her nostrils closed. She could not breathe. Dear God, she could not breathe!

She flailed against him. Tried to bring her legs up to do some damage, any damage.

And he laughed. "Go on and expend yourself. It will make this quicker. Then Lord Lucien bloody Harlington will have another lover who has hanged herself from the drapery ties and I'll have the shipping business that always should have been mine."

Her lungs screamed for air. She did everything in her power to get free of Gerald, but all her struggles only incited further laughter. Everything she saw began to have shadowed edges and go slightly out of focus. There was a buzzing in her ears. She imagined she saw Luke rise up behind her attacker. Luke who was not Luke, his face distorted into a rictus of rage. Something bright glinted above Gerald's head, then plummeted like a swooping falcon.

Gerald fell, pulling her with him to the floor. His weight still pinned her, but his hands were gone. She sucked in great gulps of air. The world around her began to come into focus.

Luke, now distinguishable as himself, fell to his knees and pushed Gerald off her. He pulled her gently into his arms and cradled her against his chest. "Just breathe, love," he said. "Nice big breaths. You're safe now."

She didn't have voice to tell him he always made her feel safe. Breathing became easier in his embrace. She rested back against him as he murmured words she couldn't decipher.

Their heads jerked up in tandem as Perkins and one of the footmen burst into the room. "Wha—" Perkins began.

"Your mistress was attacked by Lord Kelton." Luke's voice was so sharp it could have cut glass. He obviously blamed her staff for not protecting her. She tried to explain they were not guilty of anything, but the words would still not come. "Wake Amala to see to Mrs. Rydell."

The footman left at a run.

"Is he dead?" Perkins asked. "Should I get the constable?"

Luke looked over at Gerald. "I have no idea if he's dead or not. I hope he is. But don't bother with the constable. Send someone to Brook's and bring back Viscount Tremaine. He'll know what to do to cause the least scandal."

The least scandal? If she could just get her breath, she'd laugh. Potential scandal seemed to follow them. "Oh, Luke," she finally managed to force out.

He looked at her solemnly. "I'm sorry," he said. "I think I broke it." He gestured to the floor next to them. The kaleidoscope lay on its side, the tube curved with a sharp bend at the larger end. "It was the first heavy thing I could reach."

Advent of New Patterns

August 1825

*T*HE BUZZ OF CONVERSATION whirled around them. Luke leaned down and whispered in Caro's ear, "Lady Lucien, if we don't leave soon we will never make it to Thorneby Hall before dark."

"I'll happily take my leave of our hosts, then, but only if you stop calling me that ridiculous name. I've heard 'Lady Lucien' enough today to last for the rest of my life." She crossed her eyes briefly and made him laugh.

He'd thought he knew Carolyn Rydell well before she'd agreed to marry him, but hidden aspects of her personality had emerged in the extra month they'd waited to say their vows. "It *is* your name now," he said dryly.

"A fact you didn't stress when I agreed to be your wife." She gave him a saucy grin and went in search of Templeton and his wife who had hosted the wedding breakfast. Luke didn't want to point out that the wives of the younger sons of a Marquess were always known as Lady First name. Poor Patience would continue to be called Lady David even if her husband resided in Scotland forever while she stayed in London.

As if thinking of her made her more noticeable, Luke saw Patience across the room laughing at something Tremaine had said. Living away from David had certainly improved Patience's outlook on life. Or perhaps it was just being around Tremaine, who was always good company.

Surprisingly, he'd discovered that his brother Templeton was good company as well. Still stodgy and oh-so-correct, but honestly caring nonetheless. He and Caro strolled over to find him in earnest discussion with Sanjeet about some shipping ventures.

Since Gerald was too ill to attend and his mother wouldn't leave his side, Caro had no family to attend the ceremony. Consequently, she'd insisted that

Sanjeet, Amala, and Perkins, of all people, be included on the guest list. Luke had expected Templeton to object, but his brother had blithely invited the servants to his house as if it were an everyday occurrence. Caro magically managed to get Temp to do whatever she wanted. Perhaps he hoped to keep her happy so she would not mention to his wife that she'd once received an obscenely large bouquet of pink roses from him.

Amala and Perkins had talked mostly with each other, but Sanjeet had been in his element when he talked business with Temp or Lord Greyling. The small man looked much more relaxed than he had at the launching of *Rydell's Pride* a week earlier. Then he'd been expecting some last minute difficulty, which, fortunately, had not transpired.

"Temp," Luke said, shaking his brother's hand, "thank you so much for this lovely celebration."

"It was the least we could do, considering that Kelton has yet to recover from the footpads who attacked him last month." Temp's pronouncement was as staid as ever. Luke quickly looked around to make sure Tremaine wasn't nearby, since his friend might have burst into inappropriate laughter. If there were any footpads involved in what happened to Kelton, they would have been either Luke or Tremaine, since Luke had been the one to hit him over the head and Tremaine had both dumped

Kelton near his club and then miraculously found him.

"I understand the man has yet to remember how to button his own fall," Temp said in a quieter voice.

"Yes, it is a sad case. We can only hope he will improve." Luke waited to see if lightning would strike him down for such a blatant lie. As far as he was concerned, Gerald Rydell could remain a three-year-old for the rest of his life. Kelton's attempt to murder Caro was still the stuff of nightmares.

"I've had the carriage brought around," Luke said. "Caro and I need to leave if we hope to get to Thorneby Hall before nightfall. I'm anxious for Caro to see the place." The house itself wasn't imposing, but Luke thought his new wife would enjoy the quiet informality of the place.

"I'm glad father decided to deed the property to you. Even if this entire debacle with your mother's jewels hadn't occurred, Thorneby Hall was unentailed and should have passed to either you or David." Temp flushed in embarrassment at mentioning David.

Luke didn't feel obligated to tell Temp that while he would never forget his half-brother's betrayal, it no longer occupied much of his conscious thought. Luke now looked on the events of the past as a crooked path that had led him to the happiness he'd now found. If his life had gone as planned, he would be a vicar in some distant parish with a wife who was not Caro. That was too horrible to contemplate.

He felt a soft pressure on his arm and looked down to see his wife by his side. She'd donned a peach colored bonnet that matched her dress and looked delectable. "I'm ready," she said.

And then all was hurry and good wishes, and they were in the coach on their way to a new life.

"What is that?" Caro asked, pointing to the large package that sat in the middle of the rear-facing seat.

Luke chuckled. "I thought we'd get at least two blocks before you asked. That's your wedding gift."

Caro reached up to touch the strand of pearls around her neck. "But I thought these were my gift." Since they'd decided Patience might be hurt if she wore the canary diamond, the pearls had seemed a good, neutral choice.

"No, that was just a gift. This is the one that counts." At least Luke hoped this was the case. It had seemed like a brilliant idea when he'd ordered it. Now he wasn't so sure. He reached over, retrieved the gaily-wrapped package, and placed it in Caro's lap.

She tore into the paper with the enthusiasm of a five-year-old. When she removed the box top, she muttered, "Oh, Luke," and turned to him with tears in her eyes.

"I know the one Charles gave you held a lot of memories, but since I broke it, I wanted to be the one to give you a new one." He lifted the kaleidoscope out of the box and placed it on his own lap. "The tube on this one is removable, so you can hold it directly to your eye." He slid the tube out of the stand and handed it to her.

She immediately looked in the eyepiece and pointed the other end toward the bright sunshine coming in the carriage window. "Oh my heavens, these patterns are even more complex." She turned the object box and continued to make sounds of approval.

She finally pulled the tube away from her eye, "Luke, this is spectacular!" She balanced the stand on his lap and leaned over to kiss him.

The edge of her bonnet hit him in the forehead. That damned bonnet needed to go. Actually, it was two hours until they changed horses. In that period of time, a lot of clothing could go—or be rearranged. "There's an inscription," he said, his voice tightening with other parts of his body.

She turned the tube until she saw the engraving. *May There Always Be Beauty – August 14, 1825.* "It's perfect," she said. "These will be our patterns, forever changing but always beautiful." She turned again toward the brightest source of light.

Luke placed the stand in the box by his feet. "Your bonnet's askew," he said, reaching to untie the jaunty bow under her chin and lifting the hat free. Well, at least that was removed, but his chances of any further disrobing were going to have to wait until Caro tired of looking in the kaleidoscope.

He settled back to watch his wife, absorbed in her own task. Here was beauty more diverse and bright than anything manmade could ever show. This was a view he would never tire of, regardless of how time's hand changed the patterns.

AUTHOR'S NOTES

Historical events often mold my characters' behavior and motivation. *Kaleidoscope*, however, is less firmly tied to an exact time in the past than most of my other tales. But this doesn't mean that I didn't have to "fudge" some dates a bit to make the story work.

Caro's grandmother would have been much more likely to marry an Englishman in the 18th century than later. The wills of East India Company officials in the 1780's show that fully one-third left their goods to Indian wives and their Anglo-Indian children. These cross-cultural marriages rapidly declined and became less socially acceptable as larger numbers of English women arrived in India in the 19th century. And so, playing with a backstory that appears nowhere on paper but lives in my head, 1825 became the logical date for the love story in this novella.

Alas, I also had to contend with that pesky kaleidoscope, which was invented by David Brewster in 1816 and manufactured in large quantities in 1817. It's hard to believe the instant popularity of this device. When it first appeared, over 200,000 were sold in a three-month period. It makes perfect sense that Charles Rydell would choose it as a gift for a seven-year-old girl. And here's the "fudge." Caro received her kaleidoscope in 1803. Such is the magic of fiction.

In all other ways, 1825 worked well for the background of the love story between Carolyn Rydell and Lord Lucien Harlington. Although the Regency had officially ended in 1820, when the Prince Regent became George IV, the manners and mores remained the same. Huge East Indiamen ships still carried most of the cargo around the world. The age of the fast Clipper and eventually steam-powered ships was yet to arrive. Ten years after Napoleon's defeat at Waterloo, the world was essentially at peace.

Women's fashions were changing, however, as they always do. By 1825, the waistline of dresses had again settled on or near a woman's natural waist, and skirts were widening. Both of these changes necessitated the return of the corset. Alas!

Such are the odds and ends that anyone who writes in a given historical period must consider. I'm sure

I've made mistakes, but I have tried to faithfully reproduce a specific time and place.

I hope you enjoyed *Kaleidoscope*. Please stop by www.hannahmeredith.com to leave any questions or comments. I love hearing from readers. Also, honest reviews are always helpful to others who are looking for a book they might find appealing. So please consider leaving a review at the site of your choice.

Happy reading.

Thanks,

Hannah

ACKNOWLEDGEMENTS

Thanks to all the usual suspects who have read and commented on this book as a work in progress. A special tip-of-the-hat to Anna D. Allen, who helped rein in some of my excessive verbiage. I appreciated her wise counsel but chose to ignore the proliferation of dangling modifiers. Those are all mine.

Also by Hannah Meredith

Kestrel

A Dangerous Indiscretion

Indentured Hearts